MISSION: MISTAKEN IDENTITY

by Michelle Janene

STRONG TOWER
PRESS

Sacramento

Strong Tower Press
PO Box 232901
Sacramento, CA 95823 USA
http://strongtowerpress.com

Publishers note: This is a work of fiction.
Names, characters, places and incidents are either
products of the author's imagination or used factiously.
All characters are fictional, and any
Similarity to people living or dead is entirely coincidental.

Cover art by D's Designs

ISBN: 978-1-942320-01-2

Printed in the United States of America

To Almighty God,
For the gift of words.

To Jon and Sharon Murray,
Your unconditional love and
support overwhelm me daily.

To Danielle Whetstone
For wrapping my words in beauty.

To Jane, Lori, and Mary,
Writing sisters, who share our love for God,
words, and laughter.
You inspire me.

1 The Grab

A massive hand clamped over Samantha's mouth, startling her awake. A steel arm rammed under her back and fastened around her waist. Jerked from her bed, Samantha found herself sitting between her attacker's knees, her back pressed tight to a hard chest, as a warm Irish tinted whisper hissed over her ear. "Don't be fightin'. I'm here to be savin' ye."

She pounded against the man's massive thighs with her fists, but like slugging a concrete wall, it only served to hurt her hands. Samantha clawed at the massive paw fixed over her mouth. Twisting and turning she struggled to maneuver her feet for more leverage.

Sitting on the floor, her assailant twisted, maneuvering his body between her and the bed. Still held in her capture's grasp, his chest pressed against her back. He hunched her over her knees with her face pressed near the floor. Samantha fought to breath crushed under his weight. Breathing grew impossible as bullets shattered glass and thudded through walls around them.

Samantha froze—air became trapped in her lungs and burned her insides. Her captor flinched and a sharp intake of air flew by her ear with a muddled curse.

The bullets rained down like a heavy winter storm

—unending and deadly. She turned to stone in her captor's grasp. Her mind raced, fighting to understand what was happening. *Lord, help me.*

The gunfire abated. Her human-shield jerked her up. Feet dangling above the carpet, she couldn't stop him. Samantha remained locked in the beast's iron embrace as they moved across the hall to the office on the back area of the house.

Her feet landed on the hard cool tiles. She stomped on his foot and jerked to free herself.

He tightened his hold.

She couldn't thrash, or twist anything but her arms. It even hurt to breathe.

Words ground out from the mouth pressed against her ear. "For cryin' out loud, Samantha, I'm tryin' to help ye. Would ye be still—"

She elbowed him cutting off his next words. *I don't recognize his voice. How does he know my name?*

A bullet passed through the width of the house, out the window in front of her, leaving a hole surrounded by mirrored rings of cracks in the dual panes. Samantha stilled, noting no refection from the other windowpane. The blinds were opened all the way, but the reflection-less window was not slid open. Both panes were gone. This explained her attacker entering without triggering the alarm. She would invest in glass alarms—if she lived.

Please, Lord, save me.

More glass shattered. The security screen at the front door rattled, banged, and more crashing.

The steel beam around her waist loosened and she fought for freedom.

"Sam!" he barked, and his arm returned to encircle her—now around her neck. Her chin nestled in the crook of his elbow. "We have to be getting' out of here —now—and if ye won't be comin' willin'…"

The monster's hold tightened. Samantha fought for breath and clawed at the sweatshirt-covered arm. She stifled her fear and stilled. *Lord, please.* His hold remained. Darkness descended, closing in from the edges of her vision. Her mind muddled. Blackness…

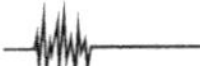

Consciousness returned in jolts of pain. Her captor ran with her slung over his shoulder like one of her students' backpacks. She kicked at the arm held over her calves and slammed both fists into his back with a shriek. "Let me go!"

In less than half a heartbeat, Samantha lay flat on her back on the ground. His hand again clamped over her mouth. He lay on top of her, pinning her arms between them and holding her legs still with the weight of his own. Waning moonlight reflected in his eyes, revealing the fear in them as his gaze darted from her to everything in the surrounding area.

Heavy footfalls crunched autumn leaves. He went rigid and held her immobile on the ground between two homes. Facial hair rubbed her cheek. "Don't be makin' a sound."

She didn't dare breathe as the silhouette of a hulk passed a few feet away, the outline of his enormous weapon held at the ready in his hands.

She quaked, the ground scraping against her skin through her thin pajamas.

The gun-toting silhouette walked along the fence line and toward the other side of the house in the direction they had come.

"Come out, Paddy, por favor," the shadow growled. "You two have nowhere to run, amigo. Give up."

Like sculpted marble, Paddy's muscle tensed, but he didn't move. A near inaudible growl tickled her ear.

"Stop yapping, estúpido." Another shadow entered the yard near the first. "Ol' Paddy's too stubborn to let us shoot them without a fight."

The two gun-packing apparitions faded into the night. Paddy still didn't move. As the sound of the hunters faded, the chill from the ground spread through the thin satin covering Samantha's body. She noticed her tennis shoes now hang from around Paddy's neck and resting on her shoulders.

"Alright Sam, this is how it be."

She shifted her gaze to meet Paddy's hard glare.

"I can't be fightin' ye with them so close. Ye see they mean to kill us both, don't ye?"

Huh? What had she done to warrant gunmen hunting her?

"I am truly sorry, Luv. If I hadn't stopped for coffee…"

He let his words trail and she stared at him trying to recall the few hours since the previous morning. Like a movie playing in reverse, her mind whirled back over the day. Chinese takeout for dinner, grading papers before leaving school, teaching…coffee?

No, not coffee—hot chocolate. She stopped before school to pick up a gift card for a coworker's birthday and treated herself to a little liquid breakfast. The line was long. Collecting her drink at last, she whirled, running into a man, covering him in chocolate— thankfully she'd ordered white chocolate.

Her focus returned to the man holding her to the cold ground. Recognition dawned—the man she covered in chocolate.

"Luv, ye be havin' three choices." The lilt of his whisper tickled her ears. "I'll be removin' me hand now. Ye can scream and those gun-wielding men will be cuttin' us down before we stand. Ye can run, but don't ye be doubtin' they'll be gettin' ye. They won't kill ye 'til they get what they want, but since ye be knowin' nothin', they'll torture ye 'til ye die." He held her gaze with his earnest plea. "Or, Luv, ye can be trustin' I'll get ye out of this mess and come with me."

Paddy shifted to his knees. "Be makin' yer choice, Lassie." He rose, releasing her.

Samantha watched him from the flat of her back.

He reached out his hand for her.

She rolled from him and rose on trembling legs. She stared at his dark form with only a sliver of the moon to illuminate the night. He snatched something from the ground nearby and handed her the soft lump she couldn't distinguish. Separating the bundle, she found a pair of baggy sweatpants and a hoodie. She slipped them over her pajamas and he passed her the shoes. She searched inside each toe hoping for socks. Samantha hated wearing shoes without something soft between her skin and the sweaty inside. Yanking the laces loose she dropped them on the ground, shoved each foot inside, and knelt to tie the laces. As she rose, he again offered his hand. Confusion, doubt, and fear filled her limbs with the lead of indecision.

Leaves rustled and she turned toward the noise. A vise-grip clamped down around her wrist and propelled her forward. Struggling to get her feet under her as they flew through yards and in between parked cars, she stumbled along behind Paddy. Hero or kidnapper, she still didn't know, but he appeared the better alternative to the gun-packing behemoths tracking them.

A dog barked a few houses back. A muffled pop sounded, followed by a weak yap and then silence. An involuntary yelp burst from Samantha's lips.

A flurry of bullets spewed in their general direction. Paddy threw her down behind an oversized van. Car alarms blared. Yard lights popped on, spreading light on both hunters and prey. Paddy drew a small handgun from his back and returned fire. The cacophony of gunshots and pinging bullets thundered around her. Somewhere a man moaned in the night and the oncoming rain of terror diminished. Sirens cried out their approach.

Paddy fired until his gun clicked with each trigger pull. He cursed, grabbed her hand, and started running again. They ducked into the shadows as law enforcement flooded the street.

One black and white slowed, stopping not far away. Samantha tore from Paddy's grasp and moved toward it. Stepping into her path and staring directly into her eyes, his head jerked side to side slowly. He stood only inches taller than her, but his clothes stretched tight over thick muscles. "They will be gettin' to ye easiest if ye're in custody. They have more on the inside thans on the outside, Luv." He put his hand out again.

Far off shouts filled the air and more gunfire erupted. She moved her hands behind her back, eyeing the flashing lights atop the police car. *Surely I would be safer with them.* She remembered his warning that if whoever was chasing them got her they would torture her for information she didn't have. Her eyes shifted back to Paddy. *Do I dare trust him? What if he is part of them and this is all a trick to get her? But who would want a middle school teacher? Lord, help. Who do I trust?*

At last she stepped around him and moved toward the patrol vehicle, but it continued around the corner and out of sight.

Paddy appeared in her path once more. "Please, Luv. Ye have to be trustin' me. I'll see ye safe back home again soon."

"Who are you? What's going on? Why do they want to kill me, and who are they?" Questions shot from her lips nearly as fast as the bullets moments ago.

Paddy looked around and stepped closer, driving her further back into the shadows before him. "I be the one tryin' to save ye, and they be tryin' to kill ye. Now come." His hand shot out to take hold of her once more.

She jerked away from his reach. "If I don't come, will you choke me unconscious again?"

"I wouldn't be wantin' to, Luv. But I will be doin' what I must to see ye stay safe."

Muffled shouts came from the direction where the cop car had disappeared, followed by a short burst of gunfire.

Samantha took a slow side-step—neither toward nor away from the commotion back nearer her house.

Paddy stepped beside her. "We need to be movin' along." The distance grew between them as he walked away from her—though he glanced back several times.

She milled about aimlessly, consumed by her indecision. He moved toward the glowing sky of the approaching sunrise—and who knew what else. The gun battle behind them still rang out sporadically. The whirl of a helicopter approached. *He might be the best choice in this moment. When we come to a safer place, I can slip away,* she reasoned. *But what if he is not the rescuer he professes to be?*

2 The Explanation

"We need more distance," Paddy muttered as Samantha drew closer—though she remained well out of his reach. Paddy started checking the doors of every car they passed. After dozens without success, he scooped up loose brick from the decorative trim around a plant bed and raised it in the air.

Bolting ahead, Samantha stepped between him and the hapless window. She planted her hands on his chest as she attempted to shove him away. "No!" she gasped. "Hardworking people live in this neighborhood who can't afford to lose their cars. It may be the only thing keeping them above poverty."

"But Luv—"

She crossed her arms in front of her. "Find another way."

The brick thudded to the ground. Samantha startled at his hazel eyes glinting in rising sun as he scanned their surroundings, then he kept moving. Samantha followed, struggling to decide whether to keep up or allow herself to fall far behind—and find another option. The notion that she could be easy prey to whoever had riddled her house with bullets kept her close to the Irishman hurrying down the street. The rumble of a truck approached in the dawn light. They waited behind a parked car for the flatbed truck to pass. It stopped behind them and the thumping of an empty trashcan falling to the ground filled the still air.

Paddy leaned close, his warm whisper tickling her skin. "That's our ticket, Luv. Be ready when they start again." A moment later they ran after the flatbed. Paddy leapt onto the bumper with ease and brought her up behind him. They slipped between the dozens of new waste receptacles to the front. The truck lurched to a stop as Paddy sat her between the last cans and the cab. He put his finger to his lips to keep her quiet as they waited for the driver and his partner to drop off the next bin.

Samantha wrapped her arms around her legs and held them tight to her chest as she stared at Paddy, seeing more of him with each moment of the growing morning. The early rays of sun glinted off the tips of red in his spiked hair and close-trimmed beard. She leaned back against the can on the outside rail while he tried to stretch out his leg. A dark stain marred the light fabric on his thigh and he rubbed it with a wince.

"Are you shot?" she whispered.

"Nothin' to be worryin' about, Luv."

Irish brogue colored his words more each time he spoke.

"Paddy, what did I do?"

His long narrow nose crinkled and his lips curled. "Don't be callin' me that, Lassie. Names Collin, Collin Fitz*pat*rick." His head rested back against the cab as he waited for the next drop off.

"Ye didn't do a thin', Sam. I work f'r some people ye never need know. I've been tryin' to quit, but it's not the type of organization that condones such disloyalty. They be huntin' me and have put some old enemies on me trail to make sure the job gets done final like. I thought I eluded them when I stopped in f'r a cup of energy. We had our mishap and the fates worked against us both."

He *tsk-ed* and waited for the next stop. "Ye spent so much time fussin' over me and yer spilt drink, Lass, all those watchin' must've figured ye were a contact. Now they'll be usin' ye to get to me."

"How do you all know my name and where I live?"

His face brightened with a crooked smile. "Followed ye to school. Website has yer picture and yer name. Ran yer license plate and got the address."

Samantha shuddered.

They rode in silence while the truck meandered from neighborhood to neighborhood. As the sun crested over the foothills far off in the distance, Collin moved the bins they hid behind. "One more stop, Luv, and we'll have to find other transportation."

As they stood on the street, the flatbed lumbered away, Collin's attention turned to a mass-transit train whisking by. "Where's the nearest station?"

Samantha looked around to get her bearings, and pointed down the street. At the station Collin raised her hood as the train stopped. They moved to the back of the last car. She sat as he hovered over her, swaying with the movement. His eyes scanned the car looking for, what—she didn't know.

"Surely the men who shot up my house are either dead," she trembled, "or in police custody. Can't I go home now?"

Collin glared at her as a few heads nearby turned with raised brows. She examined her stained tennis shoes as heat filled her cheeks and remained silent until he led her off at the end of the route. Now downtown, Collin kept her moving from one alley to another.

He stepped out onto a sidewalk, cursed and stepped back, pressing her against the wall.

As he watched from the shadows, Samantha took his moment of distraction to slip away. She backed away from him and down the first alley. A list of friends scrolled through her mind. *Who to call? No one from school—they'd find me too easily. Church friends? No, I don't know anyone's number for memory.* Come to think of it, every contact was saved in her cell, which was back in her purse near the front door of her shot up house.

A soft pleading drew her attention to a cardboard box. Whimpered mewing and the need to tend to someone other than herself made her stop. She squatted in the filthy alley next to a man cradling a kitten. He reeked of sweat and urine, his grey beard hung from his chin, matted and caked with grime almost as dark as his tattered clothes.

Samantha smiled and stroked the kitten's fluffy head.

"She 'as a hurt paw," the man moaned with breath that propelled her back on her rump.

"May I see?"

After a moment, he handed the tiny creature to her. Samantha laid the kitten on its back in the crook of her arm and looked at her front paw, swollen near twice its size. The kitten cried as she took the wounded paw, and squirmed to free itself. "A shard of glass is in it."

He groaned, "These ol' eyes couldn't see it."

Holding her breath, Samantha tried to wrench it out, but the kitten wiggled in pain. "Hold her still and I'll get it." The man held his kitten with a tenderness she didn't expect from his rough, blackened hands. Samantha trapped the tiny sliver between her nails and pulled.

"Samantha!" the fear-filled cry echoed down the

narrow passage. He shouted again, and again—each time more sharp and dripping with growing fear. Rounding the dumpster Collin seized her arm and jerked her to her feet. "What be you thinkin'? I can't—" He cut short as his gaze met the older man's.

Samantha put a trembling hand out. "I need money." He stared at her. "The kitten needs ointment and a bandage for her paw, and they could both use a bite to eat."

Collin crossed his arms over his chest.

Samantha tapped her foot—trying to look defiant and brave, but her words squeaked in her tight throat. "I'm not going another step until we do this. There is a drugstore right there," she pointed out the alley the way they came. "It will only take longer the more you refuse me. Now—the money."

He frowned, jerked her along behind him, and dropped a twenty-dollar bill in the man's lap.

She called, "Take care," as he dragged her away.

They raced down one street. *That's more like it.* She threw her shoulders back and tossed her head. Others —she would concern herself with the needs of others. *My students.* Her heart skipped a beat doing an odd jig in her chest. Samantha checked the rising sun. Still early, but someone should be at the school by now. If they knew her name and where she worked, her students and friends could be in danger. She strolled from Collin's side again. She moved to a pay phone she was not only surprised to see, but to find working. *Can I still make a collect call?*

The call went through. "Molly hi, it's Samantha. I don't have much time. I need a sub— indefinitely. Something's happened. I don't know when I'll be back. Take care of my kiddos and one more thing…"

Samantha saw Collin, only a few steps away, wave her to come. She shook her head and continued her conversation.

Collin's quick long strides brought him back towards her. The scowl on his face caused his beard to stand on edge in places. He reached for the receiver.

Samantha smacked his hand away.

Next he tried to depress the switch hook to hang-up, and she stomped at his foot to drive him back. She put her body between him and the phone, her anger pounded in her ears making it hard to hear. "You have to make sure everyone knows I am gone. Announce it to the staff. Email the parents. Put it in the newsletter. I am not on campus and no one knows where I've gone. Got it? You have to make sure everyone knows—everyone. Keep my kids safe, Molly. I'm counting on you."

She hung up and turned to find him glaring at her. He grumbled, "Callin' a beau?"

"No man has ever been so stupid," she snapped

back as she twisted free of his grasp but walked where he led. "I called my school. Collin Fitzpatrick, I will not allow any harm to come to my kids because of you, your unnamed organization, or the death-happy nuts who hunt you. I don't care if it costs me my life—and yours too. Those innocent students did nothing and they will not pay for my clumsy moment in the coffee shop."

Collin came even with her, matching her stride. "Got it, Luv."

They walked the length of the street in silence, before he cursed again and shoved her out of sight.

3 The Chase

As they stepped out onto another street, winding their way through downtown, a shout split the air.

"Fitzpatrick!"

Collin seized Sanantha's hand. They ran—darting from street to street, up one alley and down another. Shouts and occasional gunfire followed. People screamed and scattered.

Samantha couldn't keep up. Her legs ached, her lungs burned.

Collin pushed her through an open door. She fell back against the wall in the cool dark hallway.

"Climb!" Collin ordered.

She fought to catch her breath.

He gripped her arm and pushed her toward the stairs.

She stumbled. *I can't manage to put one foot in front of the other. Climbing stairs will be like some medieval torture.*

"Sam, climb. They're right behind us." His hand rested on the small of her back and propelled her up the stairs. After five flights, they faced a locked door. Footsteps and shouts echoed up the stairwell. Bullets pinged off metal railings. Collin kicked the blockage open and they stepped onto the roof. He barricaded it closed and walked around.

"We have to jump."

She shook her head, hands braced on her aching legs, gulping air. "Can't."

"You have to." He seized her arms above the elbows. His gaze bore into her as his finger dug into her skin through the sweatshirt and pajamas. "You listen here, Luv. I will not allow another innocent to die because of me. Never again—ye hear me. Never again. Now come on." He took her hand and tugged her forward.

Smacking him away she glared at him. "I'm exhausted. I couldn't do it even at my best. Go. Get out of here. Save yourself."

Grabbing her by the shoulders, he shook her, and barked an order. "You can and you will." He took a deep breath. "I can't be leavin' ye behind, Luv. We'll run together. Plant your foot on the ledge and push off hard as you can. Before you hit, bend your knees an' roll."

She moved to the edge and looked at the distance. Shaking her head, she backed away. "There is no way I could make it that far."

A thud boomed against the door.

"Now, Sam!" He jerked her back to the middle of the roof, and they charged forward to the edge. She did as he instructed and sailed through the air. He released her hand as they dropped to the other roof.

She tumbled, banging her knee and elbow hard on the gravel roof and smacking her head. Dots of light bounced in her vision like exploding popcorn. She lay still, overwhelmed by bolts of pain.

The door on the other roof broke and Collin hauled her to her feet. They jumped down the short drop to another roof and descended the fire ladder to the street.

Keeping to the shadows, they slipped their way to the edge of downtown and the rail yard. "Isn't a train, bus station, or airport the first place to look for someone fleeing?"

The crooked smile touched his lips. "Absolutely, but we aren't buyin' no tickets." He pointed to freight cars. "We're hoppin' a ride."

Samantha stopped in her tracks. "You can't be serious."

"Deadly," he hissed, yanking her behind an over-burdened luggage cart. He pointed to a broad-shouldered man in a heavy black coat and black jeans at the other end of the platform. "He's one of them huntin' me. As ye said, they be watchin' the stations, and there's always more than one. They're like school kids who travel in pairs or groups." He tried to smile at his familiar reference, but Samantha glared at him.

Less than an hour passed as they moved from one

hiding spot to another around the train yard. Samantha watched the comings and goings of all the passengers. Should she leave him? Could she leave him? *He won't let me just walk away.* Where could she go? She fidgeted to get comfortable, but the uneasiness rumbling in her mind did not come from the discomfort of sitting crapped in their current hiding spot. Flying bullets and jumping off roofs, she had no experience with this world. But would it be safer with Collin, or on her own? She fingered the few cents she'd found on the ground earlier. The coins rolled in her hand, deep in her pocket, and slid between her fingers. *Hardly enough for a ticket across the street, let alone out of town.*

Collin checked on her less and less with each passing minute. She eased away from him a foot at a time. When she neared a corner of the building, she glanced one last time at Collin's back. *I'm praying this is the right move.* She stayed close to the wall and worked her way along the back of one of the out buildings toward the main station. Looking in every direction when she reached the end of the building, but seeing no one, she stepped out into the open between the two structures.

Before she even made it a single step, a hand clamped down on her arm causing her to yelp in pain. She banged against the wall, rattling her teeth, making her see spots again. "Well aren't you a sweet thing?" The man holding her against the side of the building opened his mouth and smiled revealing two gold colored teeth. They shimmered in the sunlight against his dark skin. This was not a Mexican but a slender tall man. "Now where's old Fritz gotten himself off to?" He shook his head clicking his tongue against his teeth. "Man's not in his right mind to let a piece of tail like you wander around." He leaned in close, his dark eyes never wavering from hers. "Now if you were my lady, I'd know what to do with you." He smile widened showing the rest of his discolored teeth.

Samantha writhed in his grasp to free herself from him, but his hold tightened on her arm until she feared the bone would break. "Let go of me or I'll scream."

He laughed raising a large black gun and pressing it to her temple. "You won't make a peep, doll, or I'll drop you where you stand."

Samantha swallowed down her fear and summoned up her best teacher tone. "I don't know what you want, but you have the wrong woman. I don't know this Fritz you're talking about. Let go of me. Now."

"Stop playing games—" The man fell forward hitting his forehead against the wall.

As he slumped to the ground Collin came into view holding a pipe. He snatched up her hand and they were running again. Now it was Collin's turn to jerk her to a halt and throw her toward a wall. "Sam, ye have to trust me. I swear on me life, I will see ye home safe. No more wanderin' off on yer own. I may not be able to save ye next time."

Collin turned at the sound of the metal lurch of a train pulling out. An eastbound freight train moved with slow jerking start a few yards away.

He whirled back to her. "If we hurry, we can be getting out of here." He didn't wait for her to follow, but grabbed her arm and dragged her over three tracks, past other waiting trains. Collin caught the edge of an open door and hoisted himself inside, leaving her behind. "Come on, Sam," he yelled.

The distance grew between them. Shots rang out around her.

"Sam, give me your hand!" His command quickened her steps. "Now, Sam, reach." She threw her arm at him. He crouched down and caught her above the wrist. She swung through the air and landed inside the railcar on the floor. Collin jerked the door a few inches from being closed and crouched beside her. "Now that wasn't so bad."

She turned and narrowed her gaze on him. Her fingers massaged the tender stretched muscle in her shoulder. It burned under her touch. Her body lay covered with bumps and bruises. Her head throbbed and she closed her eyes against the pain. Her empty stomach growled. *What am I doing here? I want my quiet, boring life back.* Tears pooled. *Will I ever get home?* She moved to the opposite end of the car from him, curled on her side, hid her face in the hood and cried until sleep claimed her.

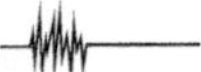

"Sam? Sam, wake up."

She twisted from his grasp, covering her head with her hands.

"They've found us, Luv. Time to go."

The train rumbled beneath her. Collin slipped the hood from her face as she rolled to her back in defeat. "When is the next stop?"

He tugged her up. "We can't be waitin' f'r a stop —they're almost on us." He moved her toward the wide open door. Rushing wind caught at her hair. She reeled from him trembling. His unbending arm around her back would not allow her to go far.

She jerked away, hurling her fist at his face. "You can't make me jump. I'll be killed!"

Collin captured her wrist before it could make contact with the fine line of his stubble-covered jaw. "No, Luv." He opened her fist, changing her hold. "Keep yer thumb on the outside. Ye'll be breakin' it otherwise. And ye don't want to be takin' such a big swin'. It'll give yer opponent too much time to block or counter ye." Still gripping her wrist, he hit her knuckles into his other palm with a solid pop.

"Short, quick jabs is what ye be needin'. Follow through with all of yer shoulder and upper body behind it as ye make contact." He relinquished her arm, and stepped back, holding his hands up for her to hit.

She let her hand drop at her side, hopeless that she could ever do anything to stop the men hunting them.

Collin returned to the doorway, tugging her beside him and scanned the path ahead. He pointed to a bend a short distance ahead. The shard of moonlight sparkled off an expanse of water and revealed the train's path over it. "There. We can jump there."

Again she tried to tear herself away.

"The trestle isn't too high and there be no sides to get in our way. We can make it." He pushed her to the edge of the door. "Feet down, knees bent, arms crossed over yer chest—ye can do this."

He filled his hand with hers. "One, two, three. Now!" Two quick strides sent them falling from the solid floor of the rail car to the void of whooshing air.

Collin released her. The wind captured his shouted orders and carried them into the night. She crossed her arms, reached up and pinched her nose closed. Air caressed and chilled her skin as it whistled in her ears and drowned out the pounding of her heart.

Frigid, water engulfed her. Water stole precious air from her lungs. She tumbled like an errant log under a waterfall. *Which way's the surface?* Her throat choked on unwanted water. Dizziness teased her brain. Panic quickened her heart. *I'm going to drown.* Blackness like when Collin had squeezed the breath from her closed in all around. She stopped fighting and let the current carry her to her end.

Something brushed her hand—and took it. Churning water swirled around her. She broke the surface in a fit of violent coughing. Collin wrapped his arm around her waist and she leaned back onto his chest as he towed her toward the shore. Out of the water, she continued to expel the hateful liquid. She lay on the muddy bank, eyes closed, and sleep enticing her as the spasms of her lungs subsided.

Collin looped her arm over his shoulders and raised her to her feet. "Come on, Luv. We have to keep ye moving."

"A short rest—"

"No. The icy water and cold night air have already caused hypothermia to set in. Ye'll never wake if ye be sleepin' now."

Her feet scraped with useless efficiency through the forest.

With one hand on the wrist draped over his

shoulder and the other around her waist, he stood her upright. "Come on Lass, walk. The movement will warm ye."

Samantha whimpered.

"What'll yer students be sayin' when they learn their teacher died? Fight Sam, blast ye. If not f'r ye, do it f'r them."

She wrestled with her own will and moved forward.

"That's me girl," he cheered.

Her teeth chattered. "Never been anyone's girl."

He held her a little closer. "All the men ye know be fools."

They staggered until she couldn't lift her foot one more time. Collin picked her up in his arms. Moments later, he muttered, "A cabin, Luv. A place to be gettin' ye warm."

Collin fumbled with the door, and it opened with a creak. He laid her down on something soft. Consciousness flirted with her. Warmth and light came from somewhere nearby. "I have the fire goin', now be gettin' out of them wet clothes and cover yerself with this here blanket. I'm goin' out back to see what I might find."

Frozen from the river and the night air, she felt like an ice sculpture melting before the fire one drip at a time. Pressure squeezed her shoulders. Thumbs pressed against her collarbone—fingertips dug into her shoulders. Jerked to and fro, her head bobbed. Collin shook her.

"Do ye be needin' help, Luv?"

Visions of him stripping her wet clothes from her body sent a shudder surging through her. She shook her head and stood on stiff legs. The chill melted and her muscle worked by rote. The door creaked open and the latch clicked. She scanned the empty room and down at her body. Her wet sweats reeked from the caked-in mud. The blanket was musty and stale—but at least it was dry and warm. She shrugged out of her clothes and wrapped the blanket tight around her bare skin. Before laying down, Samantha rinsed out her soiled clothes in a rusty old sink, and sat on the floor near the fire. She did not rest long before oblivion claimed her.

4 The New Perspective

Collin removed his wet clothes and donned a pair of greasy overalls he'd found in the barn. He glanced down at his bare ankles in the short garment as it bagged at his waist. He chuckled to himself at the ridiculous fit. *Least it's dry.* Glancing about the single room structure he noted more night showed through the plank walls than there were walls. *It's a wonder this rickety old buildin' is still standin'.* He rubbed his hands over his face. *How long has it been since I showered and shaved?*

"Ye be a fool, Col," he moaned into the air. "Ye have no vehicle, no identification, and little money. Ye would be hard pressed to get yerself out of this alive. How, in heaven's name, do you think ye'll be managin' to get that innocent, untrained woman out of here?" He staggered back under the weight of his own question and landed against something solid.

He tossed off a tarp, throwing pounds of dust and rotted wood into the air. He coughed and choked and stumbling to a half-empty water bottle. Pouring it over his face to clear his eyes, it still took several minutes for the cloud to clear enough in the dim light to make out his prize.

In the back of the barn sat an old pickup. Collin

walked around it. More rust than yellow, but the tires still looked good. Would it start? He opened the door with a creak and sat on the torn leather seat. Collin smiled at the keys hanging from the ignition. "Love me a bogger."

Click, click, click, shudder, whine. He pounded his fist against the steering wheel. Resting both hands on the top of the wheel, he laid his head on them. Images of Sam interrupted his thoughts and pressed against the backs of his eyelids. Huge blue eyes pleaded with him, whimpered cries, sheer terror wracking her body. She'd die if he couldn't figure a way out for her. Other images came too —ones he couldn't bear to remember. "Never again."

He sat back, bumped his head against the window behind the seat. Pushing the old failure aside, he allowed his memory of her to dance. Demanding money to help the bum and his worthless cat. She risked leaving his protection to stand in the open and assure her students were safe. She also took no thought for what fate awaited her as she told him to go on without her. 'Save yourself'.

"Alright Luv, we'll be usin' yer playbook. Look after ye, before meself." He slid from the cab and moved toward the front of the vehicle. "Truck, ye and me gonna be havin' a wee heart-to-heart."

He threw up the hood with a squealed protest of metal, and lifted a kerosene lamp from the workbench. Adjusting the wick, he set it on the fat fender and rubbed his hands together. "The lady in there doesn't belong here. Got it, truck? And ye are gonna be gettin' her back on her way. We can do this the hard way or…" His words trailed off at the realization he spoke to the old rust bucket as if it understood. Maybe the four-wheeled beast was the only thing to make sense of this nightmare.

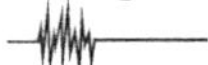

Sometime after dawn, the reluctant vehicle gurgled to life with a protested black puff from its back end. Satisfied the relic would start for him at will, Collin turned the key and the hunk of rusty metal shuddered until it fell silent. He wiped his hands on a rag—nearly as dirty—and headed for the cabin.

Sam lay curled on her side near the glowing coals. As the open door invited in the cold mountain air, she stirred. She wiggled to tuck her feet under the warmth of the blanket covering her. Red welts, open blisters, and dried blood covered her delicate feet.

Collin stepped forward to assist as her arm slipped from under the cover and tossed the corner over the wounded appendages. Her arm mirrored her feet. A long raw scrape covered her elbow, and misshaped purple blotches formed a polka-dotted pattern along the whole length.

"Oh Luv," Collin groaned.

She stretched and mumbled through a yawn.

"What's the matter? They haven't found us, have they?" Clutching the blanket tight about her she rolled to her back with another yawn, her blue eyes struggled to open and focus on him.

"Ye're hurt."

One brown brow lifted, tugging the uncooperative lid open to consider him. "So are you."

"But ye never said—"

"Neither did you." She sat up, rolling her shoulders and neck to a chorus of pops and cracks.

"This is me life, Sam. I have been through far worse, but ye…" His voice trailed as he lifted her elbow to examine it.

She slipped from his grasp and tried to stand. "Well, I may have never been through anything remotely close to this, but I didn't see how saying anything would make much difference—other than adding to your burden."

He stole her from her bed in the middle of the night, ran her all over town with men shooting at her, over rooftops and off trains. His head shook in disbelief. Didn't she care what happened to her?

She stumbled onto her feet, shifting from her toes, to her heel, to the sides before she plopped into a chair, sending dust erupting into the air. Samantha tried not to inhale, but the filth hanging in the air proved too much, and an uncontrollable round of coughing ensued. When the fit ended, she continued. "If you knew, would you have stopped? Would you have taken me to a hospital? Maybe we could tell the bad guys I need a time out, and we can treat these many sores?"

He couldn't suppress a wry laugh and put his hands up in surrender. "Oiw, I get it. Nothin' could be done at the time. Ye win. But we could be doin' somethin' now. I found an old pickup in the outbuilding, and came in to tell ye I planned to head to town to get some sundries."

She rose to her feet with a whimper. "I'll get dressed."

"Sam, ye be needin' to stay off those feet. I'll be back in no time."

She searched his face. "You believe I'll be safe here. They didn't see us hurl ourselves off the train? They haven't spent all night searching the woods, only to see the smoke of our fire by dawn's light? You trust I won't leave on my own?"

"I surrender," he groaned. "But how will ye be gettin' shoes back on those feet?"

She smiled at him. A beautiful, triumphant smile that warmed the room—and his stone heart. "I found these in a drawer before I undressed last night." She held worn wool socks, twice the size of her feet, in front of him.

"Ye find anythin' else?"

"A few odds and ends." She pointed to the dresser in the corner. The bottom drawer lay broken on the floor, filled with some rodents torn nest of rags. The middle hung off its slides ready to join its friend on the floor. The top drawer sat open draped in Sam's finds—a green, checkered shirt with a hole in one short sleeve and a well-worn pair of jeans with many holes.

Collin collected the items and stepped out leaving her the room to dress. In moments she stood beside him. Her shoulder-length hair gathered back in a small ponytail with a strip of cloth. Her steps were slow as she worked from the outside of each placed foot rolling it until the full surface touched the ground. She never whimpered or spoke a complaint as she sat in the pickup before he could open her door. *She's got strength and guts.* He'd never met anyone like her. *Is she like most women from the 'real' world? Definitely not.*

5 The Compliment

Collin turned around to find Sam once again out of his sight. For someone not trained in covert tactics, she was amazingly adapt of slipping away unnoticed. He need to stop under estimating her. He expected her to stay close to the safety he offered, but she had an independent streak that continued to take him by surprise. Maybe she still didn't understand the kind of danger they were in. He he wasn't careful, she learn the hard way.

Collin found her shuffling in unlaced shoes up a row, two aisles away. The basket on her arm lay cluttered with small items. She didn't see him right away and he watched as her gaze shifted to a side door. Collin's heart shuddered as she stilled, continuing to look at the door. *Is she still considering running?* He cleared his throat and she turned, flashed him a weak smile. She led the way to the cashier without a word.

"Hello, did you find everything you needed?" the rosy-cheeked woman behind the counter asked.

Collin resisted a snide smirk. The small country market only contained five short aisles of goods. There was a lot he couldn't find.

Sam's voice bubbled with merriment. "Oh yes. Your store is small, but it has all the essentials."

"I don't think I have ever seen you in here."

Collin's stomach clenched. He lifted his hand to Sam's elbow as a silent warning. Sam tossed her head as the chatty cashier picked up each item and input the price on the tag in the register by hand.

"Men, what are you going to do?" Sam clucked at the cashier. "He yanks me out of bed with grand promises and we are off and running. But did he make a plan?"

"Oh no, he didn't." The clerk *tsk-ed*

"He drags me around the country with not a thought for practicality—even lost our belongings along the way. Next he says we are headed to some great surprise but…" Sam leaned into the woman who hung on her every word. "Will he stop and ask for directions?"

The woman looked at him over Sam's shoulder, a scowl accompanying her glare. "Of course not. What is it with men and directions anyway?"

"I have no idea." Sam shrugged. "So, he gets this great idea to take a trek along the river to lighten my mood." She waved her hand over her marred clothes. "Might have worked, if we hadn't ended up in the freezing water."

"Oh, you are pulling my leg."

Sam's head shook again. "Now we still have hours to go. I don't know what we'll find down the road, so I'm getting snacks to sustain us now and a little something to fix later."

"Smart woman. Don't know how men survive on their own." the clerk smirked with another sharp look back at Collin. He nodded his head in agreement, for Sam possessed more wits about her than the woman knew. With careful wording of the facts, Sam told the woman everything she wanted to know without raising her suspicion. Sam was brilliant.

Collin paid with the last of his cash and they walked back to where he'd hidden the truck. As they rumbled down the road he glanced over to consider her. "Ye amaze me."

Sam turned toward him, and fidgeted, avoiding eye contact as she bit her lower lip. "I know I'm a hindrance to you, Collin. You could be long gone and safe, if not for fussing over me. I would understand if you —"

He slammed on the brakes, throwing her forward in the old style lap belt. "What be ye talkin' about?" He put his arm along the back of the bench seat and turned to face her. Her eyes darted about, avoiding his direct glance, but didn't find anywhere else to light.

"Samantha Wellin'ton, ye listen to me, and ye listen good." She cowered under his harsh tone, shrinking back against the door behind her. "Ye have taken everythin' I've thrown at ye. From accostin' ye out of bed, runnin' from gunfire, to leapin' off buildin's, and out of trains, ye've done it all. Ye've never broken. Sam, ye have protected yer students and the woman we met moments ago. Ye consider yourself unworthy of bein' saved, but let me make this abundantly clear." He took her chin in his hand and raised it until their eyes met. "Ye be far more deservin' than any person I've ever met. If people like ye are not saved, it will be leavin' a world of people like me. There would be no redeemin' us in such a state."

A tear trailed down her cheek and he brushed it away with his thumb. "You don't need to say such things." Her lip slipped between her teeth again.

"Apparently I do. Ye can't be seein' yourself clearly. Perhaps this is why our paths crossed—to be remindin' me what I'm fightin' f'r, and so ye know ye be worth the battle."

She tore from his hold with a slight tremor. Sam turned away to stare out the window as he stepped on the gas. She fell silent, and Collin didn't possess the skill or tenderness to draw her out again.

At the old cabin, she slipped from the cab, a wince twisting her face as her feet touched the ground. Inside she removed her shoes. After bandaging their wounds, she shuffled around in her thick socks, as she prepared a meal for them on the old wood stove. He marveled as he moved around her. She built a fire in the cast-iron potbelly stove and placed an old iron skillet on the top. The tiny cabin filled with the sound of sizzling hamburger, and the aroma of fried meat and onions overflowed into every corner. Water bubbled in another pot on the back of the stovetop adding a pleasant gurgle to the concert she created.

Collin filled the fireplace with wood, rekindling the warmth. In his gut—he knew better. Never stay in one place too long. But his heart longed for something more than being on the run. A beautiful woman cooking dinner for them, flashing him a smile anytime she caught him staring. He hadn't been in a home since he graduated secondary school. What would it be like to be free of his current life and spend the remainder of his days with someone like her?

Sam called to him over her shoulder. "Collin, why are these men hunting me? Who are they?"

"I told ye, they be after me and believe ye know me. They be hopin' to get information from ye to trap me."

"But why can't we just tell them that I don't know you?" She set dented metal camping plates on the table after washing them free of thick dust.

Collin took the silverware from her and placed it near the plates. "They wouldn't be believin' ye. They be not the nice kind of men ye know."

"Who are they? What do they want with you?"

"I've been bad f'r their business."

She deposited cooked noodles into a chipped bowl and poured sauce over the top. "What business is that?" She tossed it together for a moment before bringing it to the table. "I didn't think to ask, but I hope you like spaghetti? It's the only thing I can make without a recipe."

"It smells quite wonderful, Sam." His stomach growled and he smiled at her as his heart pounded in his chest.

"So what business have you been bad for, Collin?"

"They be criminals, Sam."

"I may be a simple teacher, Collin, but I'm not stupid. I know they're criminals, they're trying to kill us —kind of illegal in any country. You're not American so you're not FBI. You're in the US so you're not MI-5— England's counterpart to our FBI, right? They only work nationally?"

He nodded.

"So I'm thinking you have to be MI-6, right? Spies—the British CIA."

"Not quite." He took a bite and ate it while considering his next words. "Its real name is the SIS— Secret Intelligence Service."

She raised a brow at him.

"But it's not like the James Bond movies. The people who work for what ye call MI-6 or the SIS be diplomats. They be in foreign countries legally. They may collect data, or pass on information, but they don't usually carry weapons or stop any crimes. For that, they will be callin' in men like me. I'm SRR—Special Reconnaissance Regiment. We're special forces much like yer black ops boys and the SEALS."

Sam nodded as she listened intently.

"We be gettin' called in to do the jobs that need a more hands-on approach."

"So what did you put your hands on to cause them to track you around the world to hunt you down?"

Collin filled his mouth full of noodles and rich sauce. How much more did he dare tell her? She had already figured out his occupation, and she'd stayed with him. *Did she reconsider leavin' now?* Would she stay knowing the number of people he'd killed? *Assassin.* Could she accept that?

Her gaze held his, a fork-full hung near her mouth as she waited for him to respond.

"Drugs, human traffickin', mass-murder, terrorist attacks, any number of criminal ventures. Whatever's makin' money at the highest human cost—that be their business."

She finished her bite before pressing for more.

"So you have interfered with their business in the past, but now you're in the U.S. and clearly not a threat—at the moment. Why come after you now?"

"Me supervisor gave me orders. I refused. She sent word to these organizations pin-pointing me whereabouts as punishment."

"What did she want you to do?"

He couldn't tell her he was supposed to kill the leader of Andorra and his entire family. She would never understand the killing of children. It would lead her to ask if he had ever killed bairns before. He would not tell her the truth of the monster he had become.

"Sam, all ye be needin' to know is I have the skill to be keepin' us alive, and I no longer have the support of me agency to help us."

"You've gone rogue, as they say?"

"How do you be knowin' so much?"

"I read and watch a lot of TV, I guess."

Their meal concluded, Samantha shrugged as she hobbled up and reached for his plate.

"I'll get some more wood," Collin mumbled. "You may want to be getting' a little sleep, but we should be movin' by dark. Hate to be stayin' in one place too long." An odd nervousness crawled across his skin. *Perhaps we should go now?*

6 The Loss of Innocence

Collin approached the back door, his arms full of wood.

Thud.

Collin's head shot up and he dropped his load. It clattered to the ground, smashing a few toes and banged into his shin. *Trouble. Sam!* Through the window in the door he watched Sam whirl to face an intruder.

"Freeze! Get your hands up!" the muffled order filtered through the thin door. Collin fumbled with the ill-fitting doorknob. *Have to get to Sam.*

Sam released the bowl in her hands, the shattered glass spraying the floor with red sauce—though Collin envisioned it was her spilled blood. He wrenched the knob around and jerked open the thin wood barring his way. He rushed toward Sam as she raised her hands in surrender.

"You're trespassing—"

The air erupted with pings and thuds as bullets riddled the cabin. A hollow thud sounded near the front door. Collin tackled Sam, knocking her to the floor behind the kitchen wall. Windows shattered. A bullet hit the pot on the stove, sending it crashing to the floor inches from her head. Wood splintered.

Collin tried to cover Sam with his own body, but

she jerked away from him. "The officer…" she stammered, crawling toward the front room.

Collin hauled her back, seeing the pool of blood near the fallen sheriff's head. "Sam, ye can't help him. He's already gone."

She continued to fight him. "You can't know for sure."

"His blood be spattered all over the front of ye. There's no way he survived."

Footsteps creaked across the porch as the gunfire fell silent. Collin leapt for the officer's gun and fired repeatedly at the door and the windows. A black-clad body fell through the front window and draped over the sill.

Sam gasped. "Now they'll think we killed the sheriff." She pointed at the gun in Collin's hand and covered her mouth with her other hand. She crawled toward the back door.

Collin sighed, wiped the gun with his shirt and placed it in the lawman's still hand. He crawled to the fallen gunman, taking his automatic weapon as more bullets bombarded the cabin. Collin returned fire and followed Sam, who lay on the threshold of the backdoor with her hands over her head. He grabbed her arm, yanked her to her feet, and headed outside. He dropped her in a safe spot and moved to the front of the cabin, firing at any movement or sound. For several heartbeats the forest filled with the exchanged gunfire.

Sam screamed.

Collin whirled. He fired twice and dropped the man hovering over her. The combatant fell at her feet. Blood oozed from his temple as he stared with dead eyes. Sam leapt to her feet, staring at the gruesome image for another moment before she turned and vomited.

Collin grabbed her hand and dragged her around the cabin toward the sheriff's jeep. She jerked free and staggered back from the bodies lying all around them. Again she lost more precious food in the blood stained dust.

"Come Sam. We got to go."

She shook her head and backed away from the jeep—and him.

Collin scanned the area. "There." He pointed to one of the two black SUVs in the tree line. "We'll take one of theirs." He didn't wait for her to agree, but seized her hand and dragged her to the vehicle. He picked her up and put in her the front seat, eyes big as baseballs. Every part of her trembled and sweat beaded on her face even in the chill air.

Collin belted her in and roared down the road, not sure if any gunmen remained alive to give chase, and not daring enough to stay and find out.

Sam sat with her head hanging to her chest, eyes closed. Drying tears still glistened on her cheeks when the sun filtered through the trees and flooded the car. She didn't move. She didn't speak. Collin careened from one narrow country lane to another, swerving around cars.

"He might have a family." Sam groaned, winding a bit of hair around her finger as they came out of the dense forest onto an open stretch of straight road.

Collin slowed to avoid being stopped by the local sheriff—though he suspected that the local sheriff lay dead in the cabin. He didn't tell Sam he remembered the glint of gold on the fallen officer's ring finger. "It's certainly possible."

"He's dead and it's all my fault." The tip of her finger turned blue where she spun her hair around it tighter and tighter.

Collin seized Sam's hand in his own, freeing it from its entanglement. He spoke rubbing her hand with his thumb, his voice shaking. "Ye've done nothin' wrong, Sam."

Her head shook back in forth in small slow movements as fresh tears wet her pale face.

Why was a crying woman so unnerving?

"You knew we should have moved on. They're relentless. We can't escape them. It isn't safe. But you allowed me a moment of normalcy, and it cost a good man his life."

Collin squeezed her hand tighter, willing her to hear him. "Ye listen here. None of this be yer fault. Not a single bullet, injury, and definitely not the sheriff's death. The men huntin' ye be evil. They'll stop at nothin' to get to ye so they can get to me."

She tore from him, tears cascading down her cheeks. "It would be better for me to be dead. I can't see anyone else suffer for my sake." She turned away from him sobbing as she faced the door, steaming the window with her pain.

"Nothin' would ever be good again if ye died, Sam," Collin muttered under his breath. He drove until he came to a sign directing them toward the highway, pointed the car toward Chicago—over a thousand miles away—and set the cruise control.

7 The Drive

Sam stared out the window at the landscape whirling by, but all she saw was the sheriff lying in the pool of blood. *Why am I here? Collin should have kept squeezing so I would not have come with him. If he left me dead on my floor would the world have noticed at all?* A familiar quiver churned her stomach. It never mattered how many people voiced their appreciation of her or her actions. No words of praise dared rattle the cage of her insecurities.

She took a deep steadying breath and released it, fogging the window beside her. *Collin is right,* a tiny pathetic whisper tried to tell her. *This is not your fault.* Logic told her the truth, but doubt ruled her heart, so reason and practicality could never gain a foothold. Would she ever shake this debilitating self-doubt? Why couldn't she see herself as others did? She was made for more than this.

She longed to believe the bold statement, but she sank back into the gloom consuming her, as fresh tears joined the party. Constant crying burned the muscles in her cheeks and stretched the tendons in her jaw taut. The tears flowed without end. Her nose now raw, and the rag she'd found in the glove box lay soggy in her limp hand.

Slumped over near double in the seat, her cries stuttered her breath until dizziness swam in her brain clouding the repeated replay of the burst of blood and the sheriff falling forward. The hollowness echoed after each remembrance of the fatal gunshot in her spirit. Would feeling ever return?

Almost an hour passed as Collin strained to hear her breathe. Did she sleep? No, not the relaxed breathing of sleep—but intermittent sniffles.

"Do you think there is a GPS tracker on this car? Are they following our movements right now?" Samantha asked.

Fool! He was the professional. It should have occurred to him to disable anything they might use to track them. Sam remained brilliant—and occupied more of his thoughts with each mile, distracting him from familiar dangers.

He took the next exit, investigated all around the engine, and crawled under the car. He disabled the factory antitheft device and yanked out an additional tracker, smashing it under his heel. "That should be everythin'." He looked at her once they were in the flow of traffic again. "Why don't ye rest? Ye have to be shattered."

"Every time I close my eyes, all I see is the

officer covered in blood."

"I'm sorry about all this, Sam."

"If I can't blame myself, you can't blame yourself either."

Collin nodded.

A muffled musical tone drew their attention. Sam followed the sound to a phone in the center console. Collin snatched it from her, and reached for the window switch. The caller ID screamed a name. His blooded boiled. He squeezed the phone like he wanted to do to her neck, but swished the screen with his thumb instead.

"Elsa, ye've failed again. If ye be wantin' a job done, ye ought to be doin' it yerself."

The ringing ripped Samantha from her dark thoughts. Only minutes had passed since Collin disabled the trackers. Could the phone be another way to find them? She wanted to throw the thing under the wheels, but he snatched it from her and started talking. His eyes narrowed as he spoke and his voice developed an edge sharp enough to draw blood. Samantha shuddered as she listened to his part of the conversation—which left little time for this Elsa person to respond.

"Ye listen here ye devilick…" Samantha's brows rose as he continued and spewed venom-filled curses.

"Ye've been after me f'r months. When ye and yer cronies couldn't get the job done, I became the number one target on a lorry-full of terrorists' lists. I'd reached me end. Ye had me and I aimed to throw in the towel—but ye made a fatal mistake, ye—" another vile word flew. Sam wanted to cover her ears. Her students never dared use such colorful vocabulary—at least not while she remained within earshot.

She took a deep breath and tried to put his heated ranting out of her mind. The windows on his side of the vehicle fogged as the air outside cooled and what escaped his mouth raged. Another threat exploded from him. Her breath caught in her throat until she nearly choked on it.

"Ye had me 'til ye tried to use the woman to get to me. Ye be such a fool. Even after ordering me around f'r five years ye don't have a bloomin' clue what makes me tick. Now ye've a war on yer hands, Elsa. I *will* kill every last one of ye. Yer days be numbered."

The window hummed open, a blast of chilled evening air rushed in. Collin dropped the phone on the highway. Samantha thrilled at the crunch as the rear wheel ground it into the pavement. The whirling of the passing cars almost drowned out Collin's labored breathing and the grinding of his teeth. Sweat droplets glistened on his upper lip in the orange glow of the setting sun. He held his mouth set in a thin line, and Samantha found she missed his crooked smile. Her heart beat harder at his murderous resolve and the tension sucking the air from the car.

"I think the breakup is final. Don't expect she will be calling *you* again."

Collin's head snapped around blurring his features for a moment. He stared at her as nervous giggles trickled from her throat. Collin remained silent for a heartbeat, and another.

Did I go too far?

He blinked. His speckled hazel eyes widened—and blinked again. The corner of his lips turned in the lopsided smile. Laughter bubbled up from his chest, like a pot of water coming to a boil—slow and rumbling, building until it is wild and erratic.

Samantha dared a glance at the road, she sighed in relief when she saw that they were still in their own lane of the highway.

Collin flopped back and his shoulders slumped down from his ears. He settled his eyes back on the road fading before them—swallowed by the growing dark. His laughter dulled with the light. "Sorry ye heard that, Luv."

Samantha shrugged. "I take it this Elsa person is behind all this?"

"She's been me immediate supervisor f'r almost five years now. Been a pain in me arse, near as long."

She admired his efforts to watch his language. "I'm sorry this has pushed you so far, Collin."

"As I told Elsa, ye have given me reason to fight again. Because of ye I have strength when I thought none could be found. Ye remember that, Samantha Wellington. Ye've been savin' me life this whole time—not the other way 'round."

"It's kind of you to say, Collin, but I think you would be a lot better off without me—"

"Well, stop thinkin'."

Samantha rested her head back and felt her lips turn in a smile. She would never convince him she was anything but an asset, and for once she wouldn't argue. She turned back toward the side window and rested her head against her hand propped up on the door. Though she couldn't see far out into the deepening night, she looked out anyway. *I wonder if a guy like Collin would have ever given me a second look if we met under different circumstances?* She sighed as doubts assailed her, but she searched for the whisper that would tell her the truth.

The car slowed and stopped. The sky was now much darker. Samantha yawned, struggled to keep her eyes open, and yawned again. Had she slept? She startled, looking through the dark windows to the lit parking lot beyond. Collin parked the car between two large semis in

54

a dark corner of a rest area. "Just need a few winks, Luv," he said tipping back his seat.

"Do you want me to drive for a while?"

He reached over the console without looking and took her hand again. Lacing his fingers in hers, he yawned. "Ye be needin' the sleep as much as me. Rest f'r a wee spell."

She reached down with her free hand and tipped her seat back too. Collin's thumb caressed the back of her hand. She marveled at the glorious sensation as she slipped into blessed sleep.

8 The Breath

A clicking noise filtered into Collin's thoughts as he climbed from the depths of sleep. A semi roared to life, jerking him further awake. Like an old florescent bulb coming to life, his mind hummed and flickered a few times before it became fully illuminated. The clicking continued. As the truck drove away, he noted the warm yellow glow kissing the sky. An expletive burst from his lips as he bolted upright. He dared a glance at Sam as he reached to turn the key in the ignition.

Sam sat with her arms wrapped about her and her hands tucked into her armpits. Her legs were crossed on the seat with her sock covered feet under her. The hood of her sweatshirt was up and the cord so tight he could only see her nose and upper lip—which was tinted blue. A puff of visible air escaped from the tiny opening as her teeth rattled loudly together.

The SUV gurgled to life and the radio blared on. Collin's arm jolted to silence the offensive intrusions. Sam stirred. His stiff fingers fumbled with the knob. The radio now quiet, he revved the motor as they sat still in the parking lot to build heat in the engine.

"Umm," Sam moaned. "What time is it?"

"Sorry, Luv. Later than I hoped—just after six. I'll

get this bucket warm here in a jiffy."

Sam loosened the cord on her hood to release it and pushed it back. She attempted a smile but her chattering teeth sent tremors through her jaw.

Collin tore his eyes away from her dawn-washed face and glanced at the temperature gauge on the dash. He dared remove his hand from under his thigh where he tried to warm it and flicked the fan switch to high.

Sam unfolded herself and put the cuffs of her sleeves against the heater vents while her hands remained hidden deep inside. "Mmmm," she purred as her legs stretched out. She raised the tips of her toes to the under dash vent and purred all the louder.

"Why didn't ye wake me, if ye were so cold?"

"I figured if you were sleeping soundly, you needed the sleep. And I concluded the sleep would help you be more alert. If you're alert—we'll stay alive. Thus living seemed preferable to warmth."

Collin smiled as he slid the car in gear and headed out of the rest stop.

An hour later, feeling had returned to her extremities. Samantha watched as Collin drove down a narrow one-way street on the outskirts of Chicago. They passed a glass-covered passage running perpendicular under their street. *Train system.* Collin maneuvered the oversized vehicle into one of the few parking spots on the street. A fitness center's rainbow of bold signs yelled the different programs available inside. A bemused smirk turned Samantha's lips. She had run, jumped, dove, and swum enough in the last couple of days to meet her exercise requirement for the rest of the year.

Collin opened his door and Samantha reached for hers too. "Only be a minute, Luv. Just needin' to pick up somethin' in the station."

Samantha's stomach grumbled its resentment at being neglected for so long.

His forehead crinkled in concern and his gaze narrowed on her. "Food will be the next stop, Luv."

"I'm not really hungry," she said.

One of Collin's brows rose. "Afraid your belly would be disagreein'." He slipped from the car, flashing his lopsided smile, and walked back down the street the way they had come. Samantha watched him in the driver's side mirror until he disappeared around the corner a few feet away.

She turned and glanced at the building across the street. Black windows stretched out and up for as far as she could see. She laid her head back, and her eyelids grew heavy again as a chill skipped down her spine once more. She shuddered. *I hope this won't take long. He took the keys. I can't even keep warm.*

A tune jingled from the back seat. Samantha glanced at the side view mirror looking for oncoming traffic. An big, old model Buick rumbled by and took up a position at the head of the line of cars parked next to the curb. *Don't think that is really a parking spot.* She stepped out into the street and walked around the car. Opening the back door, in search for the source of the ringing, she realized the car that had just parked sat running with no one exiting the vehicle.

Samantha pushed her hand into the crack at the back of the seat. Her fingers touched a hard, slender object. She retrieved it to find a sheathed knife. The blade of the weapon stretched as long as her hand—wrist to fingertip. She continued to inspect the crack in the back of the seat and finally yanked out another phone belonging to one of the previous owners. The name 'Elsa' blared on the screen. She slid the button with her thumb, "Hello?"

Collin sped around the corner as fast as he dared without running and took the steps two at a time into the train station. Keeping his head low, he moved through the crowd to the lockers. *I wonder how much remains on the pre-paid credit card I used to rent this thin'? How long has it been here?* Thoughts jumbled in his head. A flash of black danced at the corner of his vision. He stopped. Nothing appeared out of place as he scanned the surrounding populace.

He put his back to the driven crowd hurrying off to start their day and pushed the first two buttons of the code. His nerves hummed like a purring cat. Something was wrong.

He turned toward the throngs behind him. Another flash of black at the edge of his comprehension.

He entered the last two digits, barely looking at the keypad. His gaze again scanned the area for anyone who might be watching. His inner warning keel cozied up to him as an old friend—the strange prickle at the base of his skull that alerted him to the danger he couldn't see. Time to move—act quickly—get out now.

He yanked the contents from the small locker. His fingers examined the sling-style backpack without opening it. Collin felt the hard barrel of a gun and several magazine clips. Next he fingered the stiff familiar shape of passports from various countries, which claimed him to be a vast host of people. At the top sat the rectangular stacks of money from those same countries.

Collin clutched the vital ingredients for the recipe of Sam's survival close to his heart, snatched out the last two items within the cold metal locker, and dashed back toward the exit. A few strides from the locker area, he fell back into a niche invisible to the cameras. Again he was glad of his reconnaissance from months ago. Holding the pack between his knees, he donned the weathered leather jacket and ball cap he had also removed from the locker. He threw the single strap of the pack over his head and shoved his hands into his pockets until his pants bagged from his hips.

He waited only a few moments for the next wave of commuters to pass him and slipped into their number with a youthful, hip swagger. Like a single multi-legged creature, they walked to the exit past two South Africans and a Columbian Collin recognized. How many different groups hunted him each seeking revenge?

Once out on the street the beastlike crowd fractured into smaller offspring heading in every direction. Collin hesitated for a moment. *Head back to Sam and protect her—Or flee in the opposite direction and lead them away?* Indecision cost him.

"There!" a deep voice bellowed above the den.

Lead them away.

9 The Revelation

"Samantha? Samantha Wellington, is that you?"

"Yeah," Sam said absently to the frantic voice of Collin's supervisor on the other end of the call.

"Miss Wellington, dear. Are you quite all right? I have been beside myself." The British accented words tumbled against Samantha's ear in rapid succession.

"Uh huh." Samantha continued to hear Elsa prattle on, but the idling car captured her attention. Three men exited wearing long coats and bike helmets.

People are so weird. Why would anyone wear a motorcycle helmet in a car?

On man remained in the car. He sat alone behind the wheel, two cars ahead of their SUV. The man wore a dark sweatshirt—the hood up—staring after the others as they crossed the street.

"Miss Wellington, can you get away?"

Samantha ignored Elsa as her gaze shifted over the hood of the SUV in the same direction. A bank occupied the opposite corner.

Air caught in her lungs and her heart skittered to an odd beat in her chest. *Hooded guy, idling car, helmets, and rain slickers, bank. This is a robbery!*

"Miss Wellington, my people have been looking all over for you. Where is Agent Fitzpatrick? Can you talk?"

"Huh?" Samantha hummed vaguely. *How do I stop a bank robbery? Call the police.* She lowered the phone from her ear and raised a finger to end the call with Collin's boss and dial 911. She hesitated. *Collin said I wouldn't be safe with the police. People were looking for them.* She turned to see if Collin was returning. He would know what to do. But Collin wasn't there.

She turned back to the bank, looked down at the phone, and to the getaway driver and the bank again. *What do the authorities do in the movies?* A menagerie of cinematic clips flickered through her thoughts. Go up, yank the criminal from the driver's seat, beat him senseless, take his hoodie and climb in, assuming his place behind the wheel. "They never look at the driver," some nameless, faceless actor says.

Samantha chuckled at the ludicrous thought of her managing any of those rash actions. Not her normal day in the classroom.

"No, Miss Wellington, I am quite serious. You are in great danger," the voice on the phone caught her attention once more.

Samantha raised it to her ear. "What?"

"You are in serious danger, dear. You do not

understand the type of man who has kidnapped you."

"Collin? Kidnapped?"

"Yes, dear. He has taken you—for what purpose I do not know. My people have been trying to rescue you from his monstrous hands before he does you any real harm."

"Collin has been trying save me," Samantha protested. Her attention shifted again, like some high performance sports car barreling down a curvy racetrack, and she noted the knife. The hilt rolled in the palm of her hand without conscious thought, reminding her of a towel in a dryer. The knife? Could she use it in some way to hamper the bank robbers' escape?

She removed the sheath, exposing the blade to the warming sunlight. The light filtering between the skyscrapers glinted off the high polished black metal. A horn honked and Samantha startled, almost dropping the weapon. A woman in tight spandex stepped from the fitness center and gasped as Samantha whirled in her direction with the knife in her hand. The frightened woman threw up her hands and fled down the street before Samantha could explain.

"Honestly, Miss Willington, if you are able to escape, you must do so immediately. My men can come to you. Where are you right now?"

"Can you hang on a moment?" Samantha didn't

wait for an answer. She set the phone on the bumper of the SUV and crawled toward the idling car. She kept her eyes on the escape vehicle's side mirror, but the man never looked up. She slid under the rear bumper of the old Buick and twisted the sharp point of the blade into the sidewall of the rear tire until she achieved a satisfactory hiss. She moved to the other tire and did the same. With both tires deflating, the back of the car pressed against her. Samantha rolled free and inched back toward the SUV.

"Thank you," she said retrieving the phone. Her eyes fixed on the low riding car as she directed her attention back toward the conversation. "What were you saying about being in danger? What don't I know about Collin?"

"Miss Wellington, I do not wish to alarm you, dear, but Agent Fitzpatrick is an assassin."

"I know he's MI-6 or should I say SRR. Most special ops soldiers have to kill. It's a required part of the job and they do it to keep the rest of us safe. They get the criminals that can't be brought to justice by normal legal means. That's why you exist."

"Do not fool yourself, Miss Wellington, Agent Fitzpatrick is a stone cold killer. I am your only hope. He will not hesitate to kill you." The next words were whispered. "He has killed children."

"What?" Samantha stammered as Elsa captured her full attention.

A hand landed heavy on her shoulder. Startled, Samantha whirled.

Collin ducked under the swing of the first combatant to reach him. Putting his hand on the railing, he launched his feet into the chest of the next, hurtling the man back into the crowd. Yells, screams, and general bedlam erupted around him as four more dark-clad linebackers set their eyes on him and charged like raging bulls. Collin bolted back through the train terminal, weaving in and out of the oncoming crowd. As the latest wave of passengers off the trains thinned, the six pursuers closed in on him.

One seized hold of his pack. Collin spun inside the strap, coming around to face the man. Collin's fist landed with a resounding *thwack* on the man's jaw, dropping him to one knee. Collin kicked him between the legs as he landed another blow. The man crumpled and Collin left him writhing in pain.

Whistles blew. "Halt! You there, stop! Police."

The other combatants peeled off and fled in five different directions. Collin vaulted over the turnstile and down the stairs to the trains.

Shouts trailed behind him. "Stop. Police. Stop!"

They won't risk firin' with so many commuters around, Collin assured himself. Around a corner he jerked off the cap, throwing it onto the tracks. He yanked the pack and jacket from his back almost in the same motion. Slipping into a restroom before the police came into view, Collin shoved both items in the trash, and moved to the sink. He slicked down his hair. Spotting a briefcase, he snatched it from under a stall door, and headed out onto the platform again.

"Thief, stop. That's my case," the voice yelled at him through the stall.

Outside, a cop held a gun at the tip of Collin's nose, he dropped the briefcase near the man's toe. "Whoa, there officer. There a problem?" Collin fought to hide the Irish taste of his words.

The trembling young man, who looked to be recently out of the academy, glared at him. "Where did he go?"

"Where'd who go, Sir?"

"Guy, dark green jacket, red ball cap. He came running this way."

"Sorry, didn't see anything. Was in the toilet."

The officer lowered his weapon by a degree and Collin reached to retrieve the briefcase. The officer scanned him from head to toe, and narrowed his gaze. The barrel rose again. "You're dressed awful funny mister."

Collin forced a smile to his lips. "Always stop off at the gym before the office."

The barrel slid down once more.

"Thief! Someone stole my brief…" the man from the stall burst from the bathroom colliding with Collin who grabbed the gun by instinct as he shoved the cop away.

The inexperienced officer stumbled backwards, teetered on the edge of the platform, lost his balance and fell onto the tracks. The man's arms pin-wheeled as he went over and his eyes bore into Collin like death's cold stare.

A train's horn sounded its approach.

"What is going on here?" the other man demanded.

A few bystanders gasped and moved to the edge of the platform to gawk, but no one offered to help.

Collin took a step forward.

The man grabbed his arm. "Thief. You took—"

Collin whirled, slammed the briefcase into the man's chest and raced toward the tracks as another horn blast challenged him to beat it to the fallen officer.

"You there! Halt!" Two other officers yelled from some distance behind him.

The officer on the tracks struggled to catch his

breath, as he stared helplessly at the oncoming light.

Collin looked back for only half a heartbeat before he leapt down on the tracks and jerked the fallen officer to his feet. He pushed the man to the side as the approaching train rattled his teeth. The two officers appeared above them.

"Get him out!" Collin ordered.

As the man's feet cleared the edge, Collin crumbled between the rails. In the next heartbeat the train whooshed over him. The blaring horn drowned out the screams from above. A squeal of brakes—and all fell deathly silent. With the train, he slipped out from under it and disappeared down the dark tunnel.

10 The Confession

Collin jerked his face away from the Ka-bar knife Samantha held as she whirled at his hand on her shoulder. The speed of her movement causing the blade to stir the air as it swiped near his nose. Gripping her wrist, he pushed the lethal weapon away and removed it from her grasp with his other hand. Sam relinquished it—her eyes wide. A phone was pressed to her left ear. He put his hand out for it.

Sam didn't have time to hand over the phone. The crash of breaking glass filled the air. Alarms bellowed their agitation. Three men in motorcycle helmets burst out of the building on the corner and ran towards them.

Sam turned at the ruckus and Collin stepped in front of her as danger approached. The knife shifted in his hand, ready to use.

The robbers flew to a rusty Chrysler and leapt inside. Tires squealed and smoke brought the unpleasant smell of burnt rubber their way. The back end fishtailed several times as the car moved to the middle of the street. Collin noted the loose rubber on the back wheels. The car at last found traction and lurched forward. The unsteady progression was barely hampered by the rubber warbling off the rims. Once free of the useless rubber encumbrance, the car continued on its way in a hail of sparks.

Collin looked at the knife in his hand and turned to Sam. "Ye weren't thinkin' flat tires would be stoppin' their escape, now were ye?"

Sam's countenance fell as the hand holding the phone slid down her side. Her gaze shifted to her shoeless feet and her cheeks colored.

He didn't intend to admonish her. He regretted it as the look on her face elicited an unusual ache in his heart. He reached out a hand to lay it on her arm, but she shied away from him.

"I thought it might make them easier to catch. Should I have done nothing?"

Collin shook his head. "No Luv, ye couldn't well sit and do nothin'."

Sirens shrieked toward them. Collin grabbed her arm and turned her toward the car. Before he could open a door, cop cars littered the narrow street. Their vehicle sat blocked off from any movement. He led her to the alley and encouraged her to run. "Come on Luv. We have to get away from here before they see us."

Sam raised the phone to her ear again. "Elsa, I'm not buying it. I'm far safer with Collin than I'd ever be with you or any of the monsters you employ." She dropped the phone on the sidewalk and stomped on it with her barefoot. After a satisfactory crunch she scooped up the useless device and threw it in a nearby trashcan.

Collin reached for her again as the street filled with officers. She recoiled from his touch, and stared at him for a long moment before she moved to follow. They ran through the dark alley, Sam two steps behind. Emerging out into the street on the far side Collin spotted one of the South Africans. He retreated, pushing Sam back into the shadows. The man settled into a dark sedan and moved into traffic.

Collin leaned against the wall and released the air held in his lungs. His head rested on the cold brick, and he allowed his eyes to close.

"Have you killed children, Collin?"

He bolted off the wall as if it bit into his flesh. He stared at her. Her gaze searched his face as one might look for a dropped gem. "Elsa," he groaned. *What should I be tellin' Sam? The truth? A clever half-truth?* Collin shook himself. Honesty would be the only thing Sam would accept—no matter how terrible, the truth would be better than a lie.

"Aye, Luv. A child has died at me hands."

"Only one?"

"That one is far too many."

She considered him for a few moments. "Will you tell me what happened?"

Collin felt the heat of shame rise to his cheeks. He

couldn't meet her gaze. He turned his back to her and stared out at the busy street. "Ye sure ye want to be knowin' the kind of man I be, Sam?"

"I think I already know the manner of man you are Collin, but I'd like to know what happened, if you can speak of it."

"There be oft times when I'm called upon to kill people, Sam." Collin sighed, feeling the weight of his burden like an elephant chose this moment to sit upon him.

"But this was different?" Sam's words coaxed the story from him.

Collin turned and looked at her. "Sam, be sure I take no joy in such assignments and I do everythin' in me power to assure no other suffers for what I must do."

She nodded.

He paced, raking his hands over his short hair. He couldn't look at her and his words started in stuttered mutterings. "I only use a rifle. One bullet—one dead, the target. No one else, Sam. I don't ken to no collateral damage."

She took a step toward him, though she still remained out of reach. Her gaze searching as though wishing to hear something she could believe to help her trust him again. "So what happened this time?"

Collin shook his head, "So many thin's went

wrong—can't be pointin' to just one. The weapon was lost in transit, I had to make the kill in a small window of time, and a kid came runnin' in front of the buildin' loaded with C-4 as I triggered the explosion." He walked away from her. "Flames engulfed him. He lay dead before I could stop it."

Sam made no sound. No anger flew from her lips. No gasp revealed her shock. Only silence met his truth. It filled the alley until he couldn't bear the weight of it. Something bumped into him causing him to step forward to retain his balance. Before he could turn, Sam's fingers tightened around his wrist.

Collin glanced over his shoulder at her. Samantha's focus was further down the alley behind them—eyes wide. She bit at her lower lip. Collin followed her gaze to two black clad men approaching, guns raised.

11 The Trust

With a sweep of his arm, Collin brushed Sam behind him. He stood between her and the two gun-wielding human traffickers he had dealt with in the past. Collin drew her knife from his waist and puffed himself up, trying to make his minimal frame look as intimidating as possible. They each stood almost a foot taller than Collin. He set his jaw and ground tight words across his tongue.

"Let her go. We can deal with this like men."

The two laughed, sharing a sideways glance. "No, we will take her to assure your cooperation."

The second one's smile grew. "Yah, and when we are finished with you, we'll have our fun with her."

Collin's skin crawled at the men's taunts. Then he felt Sam press close.

What now? How do I get Sam out of this mess?

Sam fumbled with his pack, tugging down on his shoulder. She pressed it against him as if searching its contents by feeling through the fabric. The zipper hummed with slow purpose, and weight lifted. The cold solid form of a gun eased into his other hand. *That's me Sam—always thinkin'.*

Collin fought the urge to smile. He shifted the

weapon in his hand, but it felt wrong. His little finger slid down the grip to the bottom of the gun's butt. Empty.

He turned the open hole toward her and bumped it against her thigh. She didn't respond.

The thugs inched forward.

Collin backed up, stepping on Sam's toes. He brandished the K-bar in his left hand as he wiggled the gun in his right hand for her to see. Collin tapped the void with his finger. The weight of the pack shifted again. The drag of her nails across the nylon fabric raised the goose flesh on his neck. Pressure pushed against the butt of the gun. He tightened his grip. The slip of metal against metal danced in his ears. *No click.* The pressure released almost jerking the gun out of his hand, then the slip of metal returned with a whistle. *Click.* Collin disengaged the safety with his thumb.

Another step—the enemy closed the distance between them.

Collin's heart pounded in his ears, drowning out the rush-hour traffic only a few inches behind them. *Who to shoot first—tall guy or bent nose? Which would more quickly return fire?* Collin watched for any opening—any opportunity to get Sam out alive.

Bam—a gun fired.

"Aaaah!"

"Stop—Police!"

Bam—bam—bam!

"Police! Put your weapons down!"

Collin turned at Sam's yell. He grabbed for her hand as she stumbled backward into the flow of traffic.

Tires squealed.

Sam's fingers latched onto his sweatshirt and dug into his arm. Her breaths were rapid and shallow. "Ye all right, Luv?"

Her blank stare met him.

Gun still in one hand and knife in the other, Collin gripped her by the shoulders and steadied her. "Sam? Ye well, lass?" He yanked his right hand away at the sensation of moisture. Blood wet his fingertips around the weapon he still held.

"You there! Turn around!"

Collin turned with a slow fluid motion allowing his hands to drop behind him unseen. Both weapons were snatched from his grasp with a tremble.

"Oh officer, thank you. Thank you so much." Tears glistened like shimmering kisses on Sam's cheeks as she appeared from behind Collin.

His heart nearly stopped as she moved toward the cop. *She knows the type of man ye be, Col, and she is taking off. She's running into the arms of the police and there isn't a thing I can do to stop her.*

She glanced at him and their gaze held for a

moment.

She's deciding what to do. Stay, Sam. Be stayin' with me. Oh please Luv, trust me. He willed her not to go off with the police. He couldn't protect her there, and he knew he couldn't continue without her.

"They would have killed us," she said finally as the nearest officer lowered his weapon. His partner, and a handful of others from the bank robbery scene, secured the one live attacker. Collin breathed a sigh of relief to see the man lay at their feet silent and unmoving.

"Ma'am, can you tell me what happened?"

Collin held his breath, Sam still looked at him searching for—for the truth. She still didn't know who to trust. *Come on, Sam,* Collin implored again.

Sam's whole body trembled. Collin tried to reach out to her, but she shied away from him. "No, Sir. We were rushing to the train. Thought to cut through the alley to save time but they appeared out of nowhere. They waved guns at us and demanded something."

"What?"

"I don't know, Officer. I couldn't understand them. Their accents were so strong, they might have been speaking another language."

"And you?" the officer addressed Collin. "Can you add anything more?"

"No, Sir."

"Wait right here. We will need to get your statements." The officer turned back toward the scene behind him.

"No, Officer. We can't stay."

The cop frowned. "It shouldn't take long."

"I don't mean to be a problem—truly, Officer. We have to leave. It may already be too late."

"Too late for what?"

"I heard on the radio that the homeless shelter on West Lawrence was advertising free health screenings today. The line must be around the block already. If we don't arrive soon, we won't get seen. I have a tooth bothering me something awful, and Jimmy here can't see without glasses." She pointed at her baggy sock covered feet. "Please Officer, we have fallen on some hard times. We need this. Please?"

One of the other officers raised his head. "Yeah, half of the fifty-third is on call today for the crowds. They're normally peaceful, but with so many in need now, can't be too sure." He nodded to his partner. "They'll be in line all day. Once we get this cleaned up we can run up there and take their statements while they wait."

The officer talking with them scratched the crown of his head considering them. "If we can't find you there, where are you staying?"

"At the Y in the Yards," Collin offered quickly.

The officer groaned.

"Please," Sam rubbed her jaw to drive home her point.

The cop relented "Fine, but I better find you there."

What? He's letting us just leave? He didn't even take our full names? Collin couldn't believe their good fortune. Sam could do anything with people. He waved the officer a thanks as Collin led the way out of the alley, to the street behind them, and hurried Sam back in the direction of the train station he visited earlier.

They all but jogged down the block before rounding a corner out of sight. Collin slowed them. He leaned in close as they still walked at a brisk pace. "How bad ye hurt?"

"Hurt?"

Collin stopped her to examine her upper arm. He closed his eyes with a deep sigh and swiped at the sweat on his brow. "Only a small scratch—thank the saints."

Sam slid from his hold.

"Where be the weapons?" Collin asked as they started walking again. "And where be your shoes?"

"Weapons are safe," Sam whispered. Her hands sat in the pockets of her sweatshirt but she held them up a little instead of pushing her fists down deep. *She must have them hidden in her hands.* "And my shoes are in the cabin next to the fallen officer."

Collin stepped off the curb and whistled. "Taxi," he hollered with a wave. He opened the door and Sam slid to the far side. "North Michigan and West Washington."

The driver flipped on the meter and slipped back into traffic.

Sam wouldn't look at him. First the gun slid across the seat to him, then the sheathed knife. He removed the gun clip and put everything back into the pack.

"Where'd the backpack come from? And how did you get so filthy?" Her tone was flat as she watched the world slide by outside the window.

"I ran into our friends from the alley while retrievin' the pack from the train station locker where I left it a couple months back."

She fell silent.

"Ye all right, Luv?"

She only nodded.

As they crossed through the heart of the city, traffic clogged. Collin felt like a fish in a very bright yellow barrel. "We'll be getting' out here."

"But Washington is still blocks away," the taxi driver protested.

"With this traffic, we'll be makin' it faster on foot. Thanks all the same." Collin slipped the fare through the slot and a couple bucks more as he slid out, stepping into the middle of the street as the taxi sat paralyzed with all the other vehicles.

He expected Sam to follow him, but she appeared on the opposite side of the vehicle. Her back to him, she seemed lost. He drew alongside her. Together they moved to the curb and started down the sidewalk—Collin consumed with calculating their next move and Sam almost disappeared as an extra shadow beside him.

The cool breeze stroked his face. He turned. Samantha was not at his side. He jerked to a stop, causing a man in a tailored suit to stumble. His heart in his ears, he scanned the crowd for her. He moved out of the flow of foot traffic. How far back did he lose her? *There!* Only a few steps back.

Sam gazed into a shop window. Collin stomped to her, but she didn't look at him or speak. He turned to see what captured her attention. Three mannequins stood poised in the window displaying jeans and various blouses. Collin smiled. "Ye ready to be getting' out of those sweats, Luv?"

She looked at him absently as though she didn't know he had come up beside her. Her head drooped and a scowl filled her face. "I'm fine, Collin. I don't mean to be more of a bother."

"Ye could never be a bother, Luv. We'll get some

new duds somehow."

Moving off the sidewalk, they maneuvered through several alleyways. A small courtyard sat in the niche of two towering apartment buildings. Clothes hung out on the line and Collin moved closer. He smiled, both men's and women's attire dangled from the line, and he reached for his prize.

"No!"

Collin turned to see Sam standing near the entrance, arms crossed over her chest. "But, Luv."

"No. I will not steal from people."

"Sam, be reasonable. It's not safe to go in a store, and we have limited funds. This be our only option."

"No. Our only option is to stay in the clothes we have on. They're dirty and rank, but it won't hurt anyone if we keep wearing them." She turned and disappeared beyond the courtyard wall.

Collin growled his frustration, yanked several items from the line and hung a hundred dollar bill in their place, before running to catch up to her. Coming out onto the side street, Sam was nowhere to be seen. His heart quickened. His breath caught. *I never should have left her. She be gone for sure this time.*

"I think she said she was going across the way."

Collin turned to a dark-haired boy on a skateboard. He stared at him. "Pardon?"

"Your girlfriend—about your height, short brown hair, dirty sweats?"

Collin nodded. *Girlfriend?* His heart fluttered.

"She said to tell you she was that way," the boy pointed toward a park at the end of the street.

"Thank ye," Collin said patting the boy on the head. He hurried to the park. Sam sat on a swing, rocking back and forth. Her forearms braced on her thighs and gaze inspecting the furrow at her feet. She wrung her hands together. At this moment she was a lost child waiting her, comforting herself with the rock of the swing. Angry pounded in his ears at his in ability to get her someplace safe.

"Here, I got ye a couple things ye need, Luv?"

She sighed and her shoulder slid down from their perch near her ears. She gave him a single shake of her head. "I'm not a thief, Collin."

"Neither of us be thieves, Luv. I left the owners a hundred dollars. It is more than double what these few things are worth. Why don't ye put them on now? I made sure they got paid f'r."

Her head rose and she stared at him for a long moment, her gaze flickering to the clothes more than once. Sam's nose crinkled. "I'm so dirty. It would be pointless to put on clean clothes without a shower first."

Collin nodded. "Well, at least the shoes. See what

we can do about the rest, Luv."

He handed her the damp cotton slip-on shoes left out to dry, and they walked along the street moments later. The traffic had thinned some with the start of the business day. Collin kept them walking, though he had yet to come up with a destination. *What is our next move?* He still couldn't see a way to assure Sam's safety.

As a skyscraper cast a shadow on them, Collin's attention was drawn to a flashing sign on the corner. His steps slowed as he considered it. Sam looked at him.

"Luv, I know ye would never be venturin' into such a place, but I'm of a mind that it would be a good place for a quick shower."

Sam tried to follow his stare. "Where? The motel? I have been in a motel before, Collin."

He stopped to look at her, an embarrassed smile crept across his lips. "Aye, but I'll wager ye have never spent time in one which charges by the hour?"

"By the hour? Why would…" She stopped mid-sentence, the color rising to her cheeks. Her gaze shifted from him. "No, can't say as I have ever done that." She shifted on her feet. "A shower would be wonderful though."

Collin nodded and stepped into the lobby. Once in the room, Collin threw the backpack on the low dresser and plopped onto the only chair. He waved her on. "Ye

first, Luv."
She didn't argue as she disappeared through the bathroom door.

12 The Fight

The filth washed from her flesh, past the black, fuzzy grout and swirled down the shower drain, without clogging it. She threw a yellowed towel on the chipped linoleum to stand on as she dried with one that looked to be cleaner. She dressed with haste, sat on the cracked toilet lid and put on her new socks and shoes. Being as the clothes were snagged off a clothesline nothing fit really well, but it was clean. She wiggled in the damp jeans. She found Collin still in the chair. His head sagging back and his mouth open. He snored in a soft rumble. Her movement stirred him and he sat up.

"Ye done already?"

"Shower's all yours, though I can't vouch for the amount of hot water available. It was a bit spotty with me."

"Don't think it'll matter much, long as I get clean."

Collin left her alone in the outer room. She tried to run her fingers through her tangled hair. She didn't have shampoo or conditioner. Hardly the type of place to provide such things. She did what she could, but with the sorry excuse for a mirror she couldn't hope for much help. She found a plastic polished surface like the ones found in some gas station restrooms. It revealed little truth of her appearance.

She scanned the room with a sigh. She avoided the bed with a shudder, wondering when the sheets might have been changed and all the activities that might have transpired on them in the time between. Heat seared her cheeks once more. The ragged chair, caked in stains, didn't hold any stronger appeal for her.

At last she turned to the only other piece of furniture—the dresser. Over half of its six drawers were missing and most of the rest sat askew in their holes. A seven-inch TV sat at one end. Samantha placed the backpack onto it and hopped up to sit on the other end. The rickety piece of furniture shuddered and creaked under her weight, but it held her.

She sighed and allowed her mind to drift to the colossal waves of her storm-tossed thoughts. Rift-currents of doubt dragged her under a pounding deluge of fear. She struggled to breathe.

"Do ye trust me, Luv?"

She startled at Collin's sudden appearance before her, clean and in his new clothes. He reached out his hand toward her.

"Do ye trust me?"

Do I? Isn't that what I've been trying to figure out all morning? He's a killer. How much blood lay hidden on the hand before her? Were they justified killings? Did the loss of those lives save many others? Should she think of him more like a soldier in battle? She didn't consider people in the military murderers. Was Collin like them?

What about the boy? He had died at Collin's hand—but Collin mourned the loss of that innocent life. He couldn't look at her as he told her the sad tale—but he had told her. He told her the truth, though it hurt him and he knew it may turn her against him. *So where does all that leave me?*

Her gaze rose to his face. His lips formed their lopsided smile. His look searched her face—never breaking its hold. His left brow arched high as he waited for her answer. What would it be like to have those speckled eyes caress her face each day? Would there ever come a time when she would not answer his crooked smile with a turn of her own lips? Could she ever get tired of marveling at the faint freckles on his cheekbones that remind her of fairy footprints?

Come what may—Collin held her heart. She reached out, sliding her hand into his. "Yes, I trust you, Collin Fitzpatrick, with my life and…and my heart," she added with a whisper.

Collin drew her closer. His lips pursed and hovered over hers. She swallowed, tearing her gaze from the sweetness of his lips to his adoring eyes. Her breath caught at the touch of his warm breath on her skin. She pushed up on her toes.

Whack! The door of the next unit slammed, rattling the shared wall.

Collin startled, moved toward the window inset in their door. A quick scan, then he cracked the door for a better look. He motioned for Samantha to follow, his feet scraping the sidewalk as she stared at his back. Samantha's tongue brushed her untouched lips, and her hand brushed her heated cheeks.

Col, you fool! What were ye thinkin'? Sam is not the woman for ye, man. She deserves far more than a murderin' lout the likes of ye. Get this stupid notion out of yer fool head and see to gettin' her home, for the love of the Almighty! He raced Sam through the streets of Chicago. *It has to end.* She muddled his thoughts and tugged at his heart. *Let her go before it's too late.* She couldn't live in his world, and he would never fit in hers. *Bein' together would only cause us pain.* He set his jaw, fisted his hands, and stomped toward their inevitable end. For Sam's sake.

"Paddy!"

Jerked from his thoughts like a charging dog coming to the end of his leash, Collin choked on the shout only a few feet behind him. *Now's your chance man. Save Sam and put an end to yer worthless existence.*

"Run!" Collin ordered Sam as he whirled to face three Colombians.

Wham! A fist met his face, snapping his head around. But it allowed him a glimpse of Sam disappearing down an alley.

As the shortest of the men seized Collin's arms to hold him, the one who hit him rattled off an order in Spanish for the third man to go after Sam.

Collin kicked the side of the man's kneecap, sending him to the ground writhing in pain. "Ye have me. I'll be going along quiet like, if ye'll be forgettin' about the girl."

The first man struck him again, and the one holding him punched him in the gut, doubling him over. "She'll be easier to dispose of once you're dead," the first man—obviously the boss—said with a smug laugh.

Their actions drew attention from passersby on the street. The two men each took one of Collin's arms and directed him back a few feet to an abandoned storefront with boarded up windows. Collin went with them, and the third man hobbled behind.

They broke in, threw Collin to the floor, and kicked him.

"Be getting' it done!" Collin ordered. "Kill me. It

serves ye no purpose to be waitin'."

"Why you so eager to die, amigo?"

"I be tired. End it."

They laughed at him, and kicked him in the back, stomach and head. He let it come. *Let me life buy hers.*

Click-click. A gun cocked.

Collin lay on the cold cement floor—eyes closed —begging the bullet to be quick and painless.

"Aaagh!"

"Rrrroar!"

Bang!

The two shouts and the gunshot sounded at the same moment.

Collin's eyes flew open. Sam held the end of a headless golf club jabbed in the gut of one man. As he jerked back from her, leaving the club still in her hand, she punched him in the nose.

The one who seemed to be ordering the others around held his wounded arm to his chest, from the shot intended for Collin. Now the man he injured earlier lunged at Sam with a roar.

Collin thrust out both legs at the charging man's shins, toppling him. He fell into Sam, sending them both sprawling on the floor.

Sam landed hard, knocking the breath from her, and banging her head against the ground.

She lay still, hands at her sides as the man on top of her grabbed hold of her head and lifted it to smash it into the floor again.

Collin got to his feet and kicked him in the ribs, sending him rolling off Sam.

She shook her head trying to clear the daze she must have been feeling, as the third man tackled Collin to the floor. They grappled together. Collin caught glimpses of Sam struggling to get free of one or the other of the two men.

She lashed out, catching one alongside the face with the sharp metal end of her golf club, opening a gash in his cheek.

He staggered back with a howl.

She crawled toward a gun on the floor, but the limping man kicked it away. Sam rolled from him, swinging with her club at any opportunity. The erratic defense kept the man at a distance.

Fear for her hampered Collin's efforts to get free of the man attacking him. His already beaten and battered body ached and added to his difficulties.

"No!" Sam screamed as she leapt to her feet.

Bam! Another shot fired.

"Sam!" Collin bellowed, squirming under his attacker until he managed to get his arm around the man's neck. He twisted and snapped it with a jerk. He tossed off the dead weight, rising to his feet.

Sam faced the boss. Neither one moved.

Sam staggered back, revealing the broken golf club as it protruded from the boss's gut.

The injured boss stared at it and at her, and dropped to his knees.

The hobbled man tried to grab her. Collin jerked him away and they tumbled to the floor.

Bam! The gun fired again.

The man on top of him bellowed in pain and whirled on Sam. He crawled toward her, dragging his bleeding leg. He captured her ankle and she fell on her rump, losing the gun.

As the man yanked her toward him, Collin got to his feet, snatched up the gun, kicked the man off her and shot him in the head.

The combatants neutralized, the movement ceased. Now only his and Sam's panting breaths were left to fill the empty room.

Collin reached out a hand toward her.

Sam took it. Once he lifted her to her feet, she fell into his arms and buried her face in his chest.

Collin's arm encircled her. He covered her head with his hand and shot the boss as the man drew a gun from his boot.

Sam startled in his embrace and pushed tighter

94

into him.

Sirens squealed as he scooped up his pack, and they fled out the back door.

13 The Heat

Collin and Sam staggered as quickly as they could manage for several blocks before he allowed her to rest next to a dumpster behind a pizza shop. The aroma of bread, cheese, and tangy pepperoni escaped around the seam of the back door. His mouth watered and his stomach grumbled. He'd promised Sam a proper meal hours ago.

She was bent over, hands braced on her knees, struggling to catch her breath. Her entire body heaved as she gulped air.

"I told ye to run, Luv. Ye shouldn't have come back f'r me."

Sam jerked upright and like a flash of lightening punched him in the arm.

"Oiw!" Collin twitched away from her and rubbed the new ache in his body. "What's that f'r?"

Her finger wagged in his face. "For getting the fool notion in your head that dying was the best way to save me." She struck him again. "You have to know I don't have a chance of one more breath once you're dead." Her finger threatened to poke him in the nose. "There will be no martyrs! We get out of this together—or we die together. Have I made myself clear, Collin Fitzpatrick?"

Collin couldn't contain his smile. "Abundantly, Luv." Collin barely heard her words as his mind wandered. *The fire splashin' in her eyes…*

She turned from him, shaking her head. She paced for a few moments before coming at him, her shoulders shrugging and her arms waving out plaintively at her sides. "You need a doctor, but of course we can't go for help." Her arms flew up in frustration and dropped helplessly at her side.

Her hidden strength.

She paced a few more circuits in front of him.

Her intense passion.

"You're a *spy*," she leaned in and hissed the secret word so no one in the empty alley would overhear.

A smile danced on his lips.

She stirred him as only a woman can stir a man. *I want nothin' more than to bury me fingers deep in yer hair, take the back of yer head, and smother ye with me kisses.*

"Surely you have some angle to play, an arm to twist, a person to blackmail who could help us?"

Lass, ye have no idea the thin's ye do to a man. One kiss—what would it hurt?— Blackmail? Collin blinked away the amorous notions assailing his entire body. He stared at her for a moment longer —her gazed pleaded with him.

Blackmail? He did have a card to play— something he had been saving for his future. Something he hoped to use to get out of the business when he couldn't take any more death and secrets. *Me freedom for hers—aye, I'll pay that.*

Collin remained silent to her assault and frustration. He stared at her with half closed eyes, though his stare heated her skin. At the conclusion of her rant, he pushed off the wall, yanked the pack from his back, and retrieved a phone and its battery.

After assembling and turning on the device, he poked in a number and raised it to his ear. "Postman, ye know who this be, mate?" His jaw set and he growled out the next few words. "Ye owe me, Postman, and I aim to be collectin'—today. Ye cross me and I'll be turnin' over everythin' I've collected to the Bobbies. Better, mate. This trip be a double. Stop yer caterwaulin'. The fee will be doubled too. Tonight. Aye, I said tonight, mate. Be ready to be deliverin' or be delivered."

Collin slid the phone off with an angry swish of his thumb and jammed it back in the pack. He looked up and startled as though he had forgotten she waited beside him. His shoulders sagged as he relaxed and the lopsided smile grew across his lips. He stared.

"We have a plan?" Samantha asked, her chapped lip caught between her teeth again.

"Plan?" Collin mused. He straightened, shaking himself. "We have a plan. But we can't be accomplishin' it here, Luv." She opened her mouth to ask for an explanation, but he looped her arm in his and turned her out of the alley. "Let's be getting' somethin' to eat. Can't take the fumes of them pies another moment."

They walked around the building to the front of the pizza shop and got a couple of slices to go. They ate as they slipped from alley to street to alley again. Collin would not speak further on the plan, so Samantha let it be as she savored her long awaited meal—even if it was on the run.

Samantha struggled to keep pace as Collin turned up one street, right on the next, another right, and a left. Had they been on this street before? She took a moment to glance sideways at him. No furrowed brows, no scanning of buildings or signs. Collin's stomped steps echoed off walls and parked cars. He never looked right or left. He moved with near military precision. Samantha quickened her feet yet again to follow. Another glance at his set jaw and raised shoulders and the words dancing on the tip of her tongue fell flat.

They marched along a noisy street—the traffic increasing by the minute as the end of the workday signaled the freedom of hordes of trapped workers. A car backfired, and Collin threw Samantha against a wall putting himself between her and any danger.

She rested her hand on his shoulder. "I think we're safe from any car indigestion."

"Uh?" Collin scanned the street for the threat. He stepped away from her, glancing up at the approaching dusk. Without any explanation he moved to the curb and whistled for a taxi.

They took their seats as Collin instructed the driver. "Gary Airport."

Samantha sucked in a breath, but he covered her hand with his. His touch was warm and reassuring, and she calmed.

The taxi stopped in front of the departure terminals. Collin dropped the money in the slot. He touched her arm to keep her inside for a moment longer, drawing his hood up. She did the same and they stepped from the car. Once the cab left, Collin took her hand and they moved away from the terminals toward the parking lot.

They crept to a spot nearest the hangars. The long arched-roof three story buildings with walls the color of wheat that once grew on the farmlands from years long ago. Airplanes dotted the tarmac, around the hangar, and terminal. Some were being serviced in the hangars, some moved to and from the terminals, shuttling their passengers to their next destination.

Collin held the phone to his ear again. "Postman? Everything ready?" He nodded, disconnected, and moved closer to the fence.

"What are we doing?" Samantha whispered as they crouched behind a parked car.

"As ye thought, I have one hand to play, but we can't be doin' it here." Keeping low, he moved behind a row of cars next to the fence.

Samantha followed. "How are we going to sneak on...?"

Collin placed his fingers against her lips to silence her and waved her to follow.

In the growing dusk they moved along the fence to the furthest point from the terminals and anyone who might spot them. Collin stopped and Samantha stared at his hunched back as he worked but couldn't see what he was doing. He shuffled aside of the small opening he created under the chain link by removing some debris. He held up the crisscrossing links and waved her under.

Samantha sighed—more dirt to the new clothes only hours old now.

Once on the other side, Collin passed her the pack, and she took hold of the fence, pulling it toward her out of his way. He slid through, dragging some of the wood, palettes and other trash behind him to hide the passageway. They knelt there in the tall weeds, silent and still as mice with an owl soaring overhead. Samantha couldn't contain a shudder. Collin's hand covered hers again.

He looked at her, the furrows making great valleys above his brows. He pointed to himself, then to a spot in the distance—closer to the hangar—where a dark blob sat. Samantha couldn't make it out in the failing light. Next Collin motioned for her to stay. She nodded her understanding.

Collin darted off, staying low to the ground. He came to the spot he'd indicated and stopped. From what little Samantha could see, he seemed to be scanning the area for his next move.

The crackle of a two-way radio blared behind her. "Martinez, you out there?"

A voice answered only feet from her. "Yep. Doing a perimeter sweep. What's up?"

"When's your dinner break?"

"Nine-thirty."

Samantha wasn't sure which side of the fence the guard patrolled, but she worked her way down until she lay prone in the grass. She held her breath and prayed she wouldn't be seen in the failing light.

"You mind going at ten?"

"Man, it's cold out here." The guard stopped, his toes a fraction of an inch from her elbow. Her lungs seized. They burned as she held the air trapped.

She flinched as the radio crackled again. The grass rustled. She bit her lip.

"Quit your whining, Martinez. If that lunatic hadn't found a way inside yesterday, you wouldn't have to stay out there."

"I didn't let him in."

"No, but you didn't check the grounds close enough to see the hole he'd dug under the fence."

The man hovering above her growled. "Like I can stop every psychopath who wants to get on a plane.

"Well you better stop the next one—your job's on the line."

The guard turned from her, kicking at the fence. The wood Collin had placed over the hole shuddered and fell.

It took everything in Samantha not to move. She wanted to bolt away, toward Collin. *Does he see the guard? Does he know I'm in trouble out here? Lord, help.* Her body remained rigid, but her mind rocketed to all the 'what if' planets a galaxy could possibly hold.

The guard beside her cursed. The radio crackled. "Alderman, there's another hole under this darn fence!"

"I'm on my way. Better check around, we could have an unwanted visitor."

The radio clipped onto the guard's belt with a snap, and a click flooded the area surrounding their passage with light.

Samantha's muscles ached from the fear that clenched them tight. She closed her eyes, burying her face in the dirt like a child, believing if she couldn't see the guard—he couldn't see her.

A hand slammed into her back and yanked her to

her feet. She squealed like a startled pig.

"What are you doing here?" he bellowed in her face as she dangled off the ground.

Samantha couldn't talk. She couldn't think.

The mountain of a guard snatched up the radio again, pressed the button and held it close to his face. "Alderman, got me a pretty little lady, cowering in weeds out behind hangar C."

"Hold her there, I'm on the way. And keep your eyes peeled for someone else. She may not be alone."

He held her closer. "Now, little lady, what should we do while we wait for Alderman?" He reached out to grope her.

14 The Package

Samantha dangled—the tips of her toes scraping the ground, suspended by the lecherous guard, Martinez, who found her sneaking into an airport outside Chicago. As though a bolt of lightning shot through her, she reacted to the rough hand snaking up under her sweater. Her hands flew out like tiger claws toward his eyes. She kicked at his sensitive areas, and squirmed violently. She wiggling from her jacket, dropped to the ground, and jerked free.

The guard rubbed his injuries as the empty garment dropped to the ground. He cursed at her.

Samantha turned and lit out across the field like a fox with its tail on fire.

The guard followed close on her heels, bellowing in a rage. Between his size and fearsome howls, the ground shook beneath her. Tripping over something in the dark, she did a face plant in the grass—landing with several blades poking up her nose. Samantha tossed her head, dazed by the impact, the air driven from her lungs. The guard was on her in a heartbeat.

He kicked her to her back and dropped to his knees, straddling her. His hands clamped around her wrists like iron clasps pinning her to the ground. "Let's try this again, shall we?" He called her a foul name as his gaze ran over her body.

She cringed and every muscle in her body knotted. Air flooded her lungs and she forced it out in a shriek that sent roosting birds to flight from trees lining the parking lot.

Gripping both her slender wrists in one of his catcher-mitt sized hands, he clamped his now-free hand over her face.

Samantha bit it. Her muscles cramped and her body lay drenched in her growing fear.

Martinez's hand reeled back with a yelp and a curse. He slapped her.

A few new stars danced in the night sky above them. Tears blurred her vision.

He reached for the hem of her sweater once more. "Now we're going to have us some fun, you and I."

Before his flesh brushed hers, Martinez vanished. Like some Copperfield stunt he straddled her one moment and not the next. Samantha lay immobile for another second befuddled by the unexpected freedom. The grunting of men grappling hand-to-hand drew her attention to her right. She pushed up to see two shadows rolling around about five feet away. The sound of fist smacking face filled the still night between plane liftoffs.

One figure rose silhouetted against the lights of

the distant terminal. His slim build told her Collin claimed the victory and not the vile guard. The silhouette of his right hand stretched out with the outline of a gun.

Samantha sprang up like a gazelle. She covered his hand and the gun with her own. "Not this time," she pleaded.

"Do ye not know what he intended to do to ye?" Collin snarled, trying to jerk free.

"I know. I know," she soothed. "He's a letch, but let the law deal with him."

Collin remained stone under her touch. "He aimed to hurt ye, Luv."

The radio on the guard's belt squawked. "Martinez, where are you?"

Samantha tugged at Collin. "He told his partner about finding me. The other man is on his way. We have to get out of here."

Martinez moved.

Samantha kicked him in the face and jerked on Collin's arm. They ran off into the deeper shadows, working their way toward the back door of the nearest hangar.

They were ten feet from the door when it flew open, bathing Samantha in light. She pushed Collin away.

"Who's out there? What's going on?"

Samantha crumpled to the ground. "Please. Please

don't hurt me."

"Hurt you? Who are you and what are you doing here?"

"He grabbed me. He was going to…" She sobbed. "He was going to…"

"Who? Who grabbed you?" the faceless figure moved closer.

Samantha shifted to her rump and crab-crawled away from him. "The guard. I was putting my luggage into my car." She pointed to the parking lot beyond the fence they had come through. "He came out of nowhere. He threw me to the ground and sat on top of me." The man kept walking closer. "Please, please don't hurt me."

The man stopped. His black shadow stood akimbo against the light of the open hangar. "I'm not going to hurt you. Come inside and I'll get someone out here."

She shrank from him. "He called another guard. The one named Alderman was on his way out to join the one called Martinez. You're one of them too."

"Oh for cryin' out loud! I'm not going to attack you, woman. I'll call the police, state troopers—I'll even call the FBI if you'll only come inside." He turned from her with a shrug. "Come or not—it's up to you. But I have to believe you'll be safer with me."

Samantha scanned the darkness for Collin, but after staring into the lit hangar she couldn't see anything around her but black. She followed the man, staying a few feet behind—out of his reach.

"Close the door behind you," he called as he moved to a phone mounted on the wall.

Samantha kicked a strip of wood over the threshold. The door closed but didn't latch.

Collin held his aching ribs as Sam disappeared into the hangar. The sliver of light around the closed door told him she'd left him a way inside. *How is it she can get herself into such a mess and I only find her more endearin'?* The memory of that brute straddling her felt like a hot iron poking his gut. He almost choked on his rage. Maybe he should go back and put a bullet in the man after all. His gaze moved back to the door. He couldn't kill him. She would find out. That she wouldn't forgive. He tossed an unspoken curse at the man and turned toward the hangar. *Time to go.*

Collin drifted to the cracked door like smoke snaking across a field. Once inside, he removed the wood she'd placed there to allow him access, and secured the door. The man called for her.

"Now ma'am, you can't just go running around the hangar. Ma'am?" The man sighed. "I called the cops. They'll want to see those welts on your wrists and face, and talk to you about what happened. Ma'am? Oh, come on."

Collin crept from one shadow to the next until he had the man in his sights. The jumpsuit-clad African American fellow moved from one possible hiding spot to the next trying to find Sam. *Where is she?*

Collin ducked behind the wheels of a passenger plane to keep the man in sight. A hand lay on his shoulder. He whirled, reaching for the gun at his waist. Sam crouched beside him, hands up in surrender. Collin threw his arm around her shoulders, drew her close, and kissed her temple.

Astonished by his own brazen reaction, Collin loosened his grip so she could slip free. To his continued surprise, Samantha melted into him. Tucking her head under his chin, she lingered in his embrace. A slow stream of released air warmed his collarbone.

"Ma'am?" the man called one more time, startling them both.

Collin waited for the man to move to the left and pointed Sam to a door off on the right. They crept toward it and stepped into the small back room. Postman jumped up from his desk on the right.

"Geez, Fitzpatrick. What are you doing to me? You know how many alarms you triggered and security calls are going out. For Pete's sake, the cops have even been called." Postman raked his hands through his long mop of hair. "I can't do it. Find another way."

Collin's gun sat at the end of Postman's nose. "Ye can—and ye will."

Samantha remained behind Collin as he held his gun in the face of the whining, scrawny man. His dirty-blond hair hung down to his shoulders in greasy waves. He looked worse than the last time Collin had seen him. He had torn the sleeves from a red plaid shirt and he wore it open over his grey overalls. Postman trembled and raised his hands.

"Look man, I know I owe you, but it's got to be some other time. The heat is on now. You'll never get out of here."

"I know ye be havin' a shipment ready to go—ye always do, mate. We'll be goin' with it."

Postman shook his head. "My partners—"

"Be nine thousand miles away." Collin wiggled the gun and whacked Postman on the end of his nose. "And I be right here."

Postman grumbled. "It's your funeral."

"It'll be yers too. Now make this work." He used the gun to wave Postman into action.

The lanky man scowled but maneuvered around the gun and led the way out into another room. The room was stacked high with boxes, packages, and crates. They marched in single file to the rear dark corner of the warehouse to a pallet loaded with four wooden crates. Postman went around to the far side, and using a pry bar from his back pocket, wedged one open. The front fell forward into his hand. He set it with a whispered bump on the floor.

Samantha moved to peer into the near-empty box. The only thing inside was a grey padded packing blanket. She looked to Collin for explanation. He smirked.

"Well done, Postman." He inspected the shipping tag, running his finger under each line of writing. "This'll do." He rummaged in the backpack again. "Here's half yer fee. The rest will be wired to yer account when we're on the other end."

Postman took the brick of bills, thumbing his finger over the end.

"Ye sayin' Collin Fitzpatrick be a cheat, mate?"

Postman shook his head. "Nope, just enjoying the feel of it." He looked up at Collin, his gaze hard and lips taut. "We're square now. I won't be doing this again."

Collin crossed his arms over his chest. "Never again."

"I want what you've been holding over my head, Fitzpatrick."

"I'll be droppin' it in the post as soon as we get clear."

"And if you don't?"

Collin waved his gun at him again.

Postman stepped away. "I'll keep my eye out for it." He looked at his watch. "Plane should have just landed. The forklift will be here in about ten minutes to load." He didn't wait for a reply but strolled away, hiding his loot inside his overalls.

Samantha slid a glance at Collin. He stepped inside the crate, resting his back against the side opposite the opening. He waved her to join him. "Come on, Luv."

She worked her way in beside him. "Collin where are we going? Is this safe?"

"Done it several times. Postman has quite a scam set up." Collin crossed his legs as he reached for the handle on the inside of the opened panel. "Watch yer feet."

She drew her knees up to her chest. Sam's muscles drew a tense line under her new clothes. Her lips were thin and drawn. Collin's heart fluttered.

Collin raised the side and bolted it closed at the top of both corners, sealing them in total darkness. "Postman has several of these crates—most usually be in transit to his contacts around the world. He's a smuggler, Luv. The crates look like wood from the outside, but they be lined with a film that shows up on the x-rays as books, shoes, stuffed animals, or any other innocuous thin'. This one he fixed special for us with the bolts on the inside."

"What is he really shipping?"

"Boot leg goods to third world countries. It's all harmless."

Collin rested his arm across her shoulders and he helped her to recline against the back.

"The first and last parts be a wee bit rocky. Once we be in the air, it's a simple trip."

"Trip where?"

"London," he said with a yawn.

15 The Unspoken Dream

A hum sounded outside the dark box, and grew louder like an approaching beast. Collin tightened his arm around her shoulders, making her muscles draw into tighter knots. His hand reached up and covered her lips. "Shh," he hissed in her ear.

The hum rumbled to a roar. The box vibrated and shuddered. It bumped and jarred. Samantha pressed her hand against the rough wood slats to steady herself. As the crate rocked more and bounced in a forward lurching movement, she pressed her feet against the side Collin had closed to seal them in the square coffin. Her bent legs ached confined by the space as she tried to stay motionless in the jostling container.

Thump. The crate landed on another surface, but Samantha still felt the sensation of movement. Deep voices mumbled beyond the wooden confines, but the thudding of her heart drowned out the words.

The box jerked to a stop—reversed—moved forward.

Samantha could hear Collin suck in a breath. She held hers too. She strained to listen to the sounds all around them. The box shifted forward and backward, as the voices grew more distinct.

"Problem?"

"Nah. The x-ray is acting up again. It is giving me the craziest readings."

"What're you seeing?"

"Well the crate of books looked like video machines. The shoes looked more like purses. And this box of stuffed animals reminds me more of a box of bones."

Samantha's stomach lurched. A putrid flavor washed over her tongue. Her head swam. The air diminished in the tiny box and her thoughts bobbed on waves of dizziness.

Collin tightened his hold on her but didn't move.

I need air. I'm suffocating. They're going to find us and I don't care. I have to get out of here. Samantha struggled to control her panting breaths, as her frantic thoughts skittered around her skull—like a jackrabbit escaping a coyote.

Collin eased her closer.

A distant thump sounded. "There," a triumphant voice announced. "All it needed was a good whack and it's right as rain."

"Yep, stuffed animals, just like the shipping manifest says."

Forward motion shuddered the crate once more and the voices faded. The crate bumped along, rattling

Samantha's already frazzled nerves. The box dropped lower, startling her. She bit her lip to keep from calling out and tasted blood. The movement slowed and Samantha tried to find her breath, then the crate tipped on an upward climb throwing her into Collin.

Nestled next to him, he rubbed her arm, but by this point her nerves were so raw, his tender touch felt more like sandpaper on a sunburn.

They leveled off and she pushed away from him. She tried to cross her legs but she bumped into both Collin, and the side of the crate. Her muscles cramped. He tried to draw her close, but she jerked from him. *Out. I have to get out of here. I can't do this.* Small spaces had never been a problem before—but something about this confining, dark airless space, that hovered under the threat of being discovered reminded her of a forgotten prisoner in deep dungeon.

"This is a lot heavier than I would've thought stuffed animals would be," a voice grunted.

"Well, we don't have to move it far," another answered.

They swung to and fro as the crate was walked across the space. At some point it tipped way back and Collin pressed against her as he braced himself from falling and further upsetting the balance. Collin's hot breath in her face increased her shallow breaths and sped up her heart. She pushed at him. His lips brushed her forehead.

Wham. The box dropped on its bottom, throwing Collin back into place.

"That's good enough."

"Yeah, there won't be a full load today, delayed shipments out of the south."

The voices left and though a few more thumps and scrapes sounded, their crate had stopped moving. Samantha choked down her fear and nearly gagged on it. She stifled a cough.

Something banged and the jet's engines roared to life.

"Just the takeoff left then it will be smooth sailin'," Collin whispered.

Samantha felt the pitch of the plane as they climbed in altitude. She was to the point of hyperventilating then the landing gear bumped into place. She stifled a yelp, leaning toward the side Collin had closed and scraped her nails across the closed hatch.

Collin's hand covered hers. "It's alright, Luv. A couple of minutes more and I'll let us out of here."

"Out? We can get out?" Tears flavored her plea.

He chuckled softly. "Ye would have to act the maggot to ride over ten hours in a box."

"Act the maggot?"

"Ye'd be a fool."

Samantha opened her mouth and wiggled her jaw until her ears popped from the increased pressure. But even with Collin's assurance, her heart still beat a frantic rhythm and her breaths came in shallow pants. She waited. Freedom would come soon. Collin promised. The plane bumped and jostled. Samantha couldn't breathe. The only thought in her head came in a relentless repeating loop. *Out. I have to get out of here!*

Turbulence lasted for several minutes. By the time the plane calmed, Samantha thought she would leap out of her skin. The warmth of his presence evaporated, leaving her entire body covered in goose bumps. Collin leaned forward. The bolts clanked free and the side dropped—opening the crate about two inches. Samantha reached her hand out the slender crack.

Collin muttered a curse.

In the sliver of light coming in, Samantha watched Collin brace his back against the opposite side next to her, as he pushed both feet against their hatch. The crate slid back a fraction and the gap grew by a hair. Collin tucked his knees to his chest and kicked out—another inch.

Samantha sat like Collin and kicked out with him —three inches.

He turned and smiled at her, but she paid him no

mind as she set her legs to try again. They kicked out once more and gained several more inches as the crate scraped across the cargo floor. Samantha drew back again, but Collin squeezed his arm, up to his shoulder, out of the breach and spun another crate blocking their escape. The action allowed their hatch to drop about halfway open. Collin pressed his heels against the rear of the crate and shoved against the other crate until the door released and fell.

Samantha scurried past him and knelt between the myriad of crates scattered about the hold, and gulped cool air into her aching lungs.

Collin stroked her back as he climbed out and stretched his limbs. He reached down offering her a hand up. She remained hunched over, working at cramped muscles. Collin retrieved the shipping blanket they had been sitting on. At last rising to her feet, she followed him to a space between several tall cartons and a couple of plastic-wrapped pallets. He threw out the blanket and waved her onto it.

"We've several hours to sleep. Won't be no hooligans botherin' us for now, Luv."

Samantha sat on the blanket, and Collin joined her with a large yawn. She caught it and yawned in response.

"If ye be needin' a toilet, it's just there." He

pointed toward the tail of the plane. A lavatory sign was lit in the panel over the narrow door. It occurred to Samantha that the plane was exactly like any she ever flew in, just without the passenger seats and windows. She was not in a lower luggage hold as she expected. "One thing though, don't be lockin' the door. It will trigger a wee light on the pilot's controls and be tellin' them someone's here."

"Will they find us?"

"Nah, they never come back unless their toilet breaks."

Samantha curled on her side. Collin lay down a little way behind her and threw the rest of the blanket over the top of them. Samantha tucked it tight around her and settled as the plane hummed beneath her.

Collin sought sleep, but the elusive creature could not be captured. Sam lay inches away, but the roar of the jet engines kept him from knowing if she slept. He tossed, and moved to a new position. He lay on his back looking up at the dimly lit ceiling. He tried counting the boltholes that would have held up the overhead compartments—had this not been a cargo plane. He couldn't even reach fifty before his mind boomeranged back to Sam.

She's bewitched me. I've never felt like this. That wasn't true. There was a time. It drifted back to him like an incoming evening fog.

Kaitlin. Oh, Katie girl, I miss you. An ache reopened in his heart. A lump rose to his throat and he squeezed his eyes shut to the threatening tears. He hadn't allowed himself to think about Katie in years. His baby sister had died before she saw six years. Collin had been twelve. It was the last time he cried or allowed himself to acknowledge such deep pain.

Shortly after they lost Katie, his Da had renewed his involvement in the IRA, during the time of the troubles. Da had forgot about him as he grieved for his wee lass.

Collin recalled the day, with high-definition clarity, the bobbies came to tell Mam that Da had been killed. Mam threw her fists on her hips and announced, "Good riddance. The man was an oaf. Me and me lad will be the better without him."

Collin had hardly seen his Da in the three years since his sister died, so he didn't feel the loss. There was still part of him, in those first few months, that believed Da would come stumbling home any moment needing to be patched up and hidden for a time. But Da never came. For the next several years Collin learn to make his own way as Mam crawled into a bottle and never came out. The moment he came of age, Collin found his way into Her Majesty's Royal Air Force. He only served one term before the SRR recruited him for work with the SIS.

Collin shook himself again. His past life held nothing but pain for him. Why did Sam stir it to the surface? He slipped from the blanket and moved a few paces away, leaning against the side of a tall crate. He worked at the ache in his neck, his insides slithering around like a python tying itself into knots.

A shaft of light from a sensor caressed the high rise of Sam's cheekbone and Collin nearly doubled in pain. Katie had looked like that when she slept—peaceful, angelic.

He closed his eyes and his mind filled with days of walking with Katie hand-in-hand. Times of playing hide-n-peek in the fields. Moments of laughter splashing their feet in the pond. Collin slid until he sat with his elbows on his knees and his face in his hands.

Somewhere over the Atlantic those precious hidden memories of his sweet sister wavered and shimmered until Sam held his hand walking the fields and dirt roads of Ireland with him. Her laughter rang in his ears down by the old pond. His lips pressed to hers. A peace settled over his tight muscles as he let the dream— that could never be—come.

16 The Impossible Distance

"Sam."

Samantha startled at the bark of her shortened name. His voice carried and edge she hadn't heard before. She rolled onto her back to look up at the firm set of Collin's jaw and the grim line of his lips. He refused to look at her. A shudder raced through her. "What's wrong?"

He waved her up without a word, and folded the blanket before placing it in the crate.

"Do I have time for the restroom?"

His gaze remained fixed on the blanket, his back rigid, but he nodded once.

Samantha's stomach churned as she recalled the times she'd woken during the flight. She had stirred as Collin slid from the blanket. Though they hadn't been lying near enough to touch, a chill crawled down her back at his absence. The next time she woke he still hadn't returned. She'd glimpsed him sitting next to a tall refrigerator-size box, his forehead balanced on his knees, and hands gripping his forearms until his knuckles were white, like a sculpture forged from steel.

Now beside their crate, Collin waved her inside without a word—or even a glance. Samantha edged in, but he remained outside. Awkward silence ensued making Samantha feel like a scolded child. She leaned forward to glimpse up at him.

Collin braced himself with one hand on the top of their box. His head hung low and his eyes closed.

"You okay?"

His head rose a little. She watched his Adam's apple slip up and down as he swallowed hard. He nodded, but his eyes remained shut. She sat back and waited.

The rumble of the landing gear followed the sound of the moving wing-flaps. Collin sighed.

Is he dreading being in this crate again too? Or is something else wrong?

Collin sat beside her, careful not to try not touch her, and closed the side. Locked in darkness, she couldn't even hear him breathe. The dragon of self-doubt uncoiled within her, spewing flames of loneliness and angst until they threatened to consume her. Tears trickled as familiar flashes of fear charred her thoughts and melted away her fledgling awakening to a real life. Not the same old, same old, but a life of action and sights and she dared hope— love. She lost all reference to time as she sat engulfed within and chilled without.

It felt like days before Collin released them from their gloomy prison. By the time the light hit her,

Samantha's spirit lay ablaze in raging pity. Only one thought drifted up from the embers now. *It would have been better if Collin had left me to die.*

This is where Samantha's dark thoughts smoldered. Her twenties were behind her and she had never been on a second date—and only a handful of firsts. Experiences had taught her all the wrong lessons and she struggled to believe she was worthy of another's time or love.

Now as they snuck away from the hangar toward the terminal, Samantha convinced herself Collin had tired of her. *I'm a burden to him, but he's honor bound to keep his promise to protect me. Soon he's going to hate me.* She couldn't stop the dragon's tirade within her as it burnt away all logic and reason.

Collin hailed a cab. A black older-style car approached and Collin opened the door.

She waited—unable to look at him. "Collin, maybe it's time to go our separate ways."

"Don't play the maggot."

Her voice cracked. "I'm in your way. You are far better off without me."

His hand brushed her shoulder and caressed the back of her arm until his fingers entwined with hers. "Come, Sam."

She resisted his gentle tug.

Words tickled her ear as his warm breath sent shivers over her skin. "I can't go without ye. Remember, ye be me only reason to fight."

Air caught in her throat. She tried to look at him, but he moved her to the backseat. He continued to hold her hand. Confusion stirred her thoughts, like a hag stirring a noxious brew over a flame. The dragon belched and a glint flashed off a sword of hope. Had she misunderstood Collin's behavior? Was she lost in the tumult of 'what ifs' again? She fell back into her comfortable coping strategy. It reminded her of the motto plastered everywhere: 'Stay calm and carry on'. She would pretend nothing felt amiss and continue on as long as she could.

Collin gave the driver directions and looked out the window.

Collin forced the longing dream aside at last, and reason returned. He set his course. For Sam's sake, he couldn't allow her to become any more attached to him. Sam deserved far better. He could not—he would not— allow his feeling to endanger her or keep her from the glorious life she could have without him.

He hit his thigh with his clenched fist, driving home his resolve. Sam slipped from his other hand and clenched her hands in her lap. He needed to detach himself from her. Collin dared a peek her way. She worried her lower lip. If she bit much harder, she'd draw blood. He shook off his misgivings. *'Tis better for her this way. Put the distance between us. It will hurt her less later.* He kept telling himself this and watched Sam slide further inside herself. He caused her pain no matter what he did. *I'm just no good f'r her.*

Collin busied himself with putting the battery in another phone. A quick scan of a diplomatic website and he smiled. "The luck 'o the Irish be with us." He sighed. Sam didn't respond. He changed their destination and yanked the phone apart.

They exited the cab without comment and a quick sweep of their surrounding confirmed what he already knew. No one had caught up to them yet. He figured they had a day, maybe two before his enemies caught scent again. If his Irish luck held, it would be another day before they caught up to him. By then, Sam would be safe and he would be off the grid—unable to be found. He quickly crossed himself in hopes God would hear his prayer that things turn out as he needed.

Covered by prayer and hope, Collin walked into a high-end boutique a step ahead of Sam. A short stop for a few quick necessaries to make tonight's plan come together, and he could see Sam safe as he promised. He led the way to the gowns and started selecting different ones from the rack holding them up in front of her.

Sam withdrew from his offers. "What are you doing?"

"We be goin' to a wee party being held this very night at a consulate I visit frequently. There I will be collecting me leverage."

Sam took another step back. "You go. You can move faster without me."

Not bloomin' likely. He looked up, forcing his lips to form a smile. "It'll be a gas. A wee visit, I'll get the goods and take them to the man who'll assure ye get home. Ye must be longin' f'r yer old life."

She caught his gaze. "This hasn't been so bad."

Collin almost choked. "Ye deserve better."

"Never had anything better than you."

Collin turned back to the rack and fumbled through the array of garments. His heart thudded in his chest. She cared for him. The dream from last night leapt into his thoughts, warming his skin and ripping apart his heart. He must have gone around the rack three times as he fought to rein in the wild emotions threatening to overtake all logic.

He stamped down his longings. *'Tis impossible. She be better off without ye, Col.* He took a deep breath, squared his shoulders, and showed her a blue dress. "I'd be feelin' better if ye be with me."

Sam stepped forward and reached for the price tag. "Have you lost your mind?"

Several nearby shoppers turned at her outburst, and Collin looked at her, confused.

She took the garment from him, shoved it back on the rack and stepped near nose to nose with him, her voice contained in a stern whisper. "Is there a good chance we will be fighting or at least running for our lives while dressed like this?"

"There always be such a chance."

"You are not spending such an insane amount of money on a dress that could end up in rags within an hour of putting it on."

She stomped past him and exited the store. A quick scan of the street and she led the way to the formals in a nearby, more reasonably priced, department store. She flew by a couple of racks shaking her head and moved to a sales corner. She stopped akimbo, "If you insist on me going, this is where we find the dress."

Collin didn't have to force a smile this time. Blast if everything she didn't make him love her all the more. He nodded and moved past her to make a selection.

"No. Running in a strapless will have it around my waist before I got two feet."

Collin paused at the image flashing in his mind,

conceded, and tried another gown.

"When's this party of yours?"

"This evenin'."

Again she refused. "I'll freeze. I'm cold now in this sweater." She ventured around the other side of the rack, and took a few possibilities. She moved toward the fitting rooms. "I'll try these."

"I will be needin' a few thin's meself."

"Meet you in the shoes," she called after him.

"Shoes?"

She stopped in the entrance to the dressings rooms and raised her leg laying the rainbow of fabrics across her calf. The hems fell revealing her dirt-smeared sneaker. She raised her brow in question.

Collin nodded his agreement and turned before the grin could burst across his lips. *She's goin' to be the end of me.*

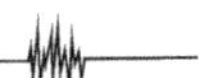

Following an afternoon of shopping, Collin handed Sam the key to the hotel room he had secured in a quiet corner of London. "Ye go. I have errands."

"When's the party?"

He glanced at his watch with a shrug. "About now."

"I'll be ready in thirty minutes." She turned to the elevator and disappeared inside.

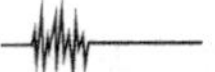

Collin opened the door. Sam appeared in the doorway of the bathroom. Framed by the orange glow of the setting sun through the frosted window behind her, she looked like a vision—the one from his dream. She fidgeted with an earring. Her hair lay in ringlets. She stopped at Collin's stare.

His heart thundered. Air lodged in his throat as it struggled to decide whether to exit in a sigh of deepest admiration or to gulp down in a gasp at her stunning beauty. His resolve shattered. Her deep red gown hugged her exquisite curves and billowed from her luscious hips like waves of rippling water.

She looked at the dress and smoothed out a wrinkle with a trembling hand. "Is something the matter? Is the dress wrong?"

Wrong? What could possibly be wrong with such a lovely creature? Collin tossed his head, fighting to clear it, and licked his parched lips. *What's best for her. Remember—what's best for Sam.* Again his mind wondered. *Sam—Sam is a man's name. Samantha is all woman.* He tried to speak but squeaked instead. He cleared his throat and tried again. "Ye're ready."

Her brows crinkled. "I told you I'd be ready in thirty minutes."

Collin struggled to breathe, unable to tear his gaze

from her. "Many a woman has said as much."

A flicker of something passed over her features, and a frown formed on her perfect lips.

Oh, to drink of that nectar. Her next words snapped him back to the moment.

"Lucky for you, I'm not like your other women." She moved to the mirror in the outer room. "Shower's all yours, though the pressure's lousy."

Collin closed his eyes and remained rooted to the carpet. His fists clenched at his sides as he fought every cell in his body from running to her. He wanted nothing more than to smother her with kisses and tell her how perfect she was—far better than any other woman he'd ever met. *Ye be no good f'r her,* he told himself repeatedly until he could make it to the shower and stand under frigid waters.

17 The Last Chase

When Collin emerged from the bathroom, Samantha sat perched on a chair. His heart went to racing again. He offered her a white wrap, draping it over her shoulders as she rose.

"Ye're beautiful."

"And you have been on the run too long or need glasses," she quipped as she opened the door.

Out in the motel hallway, Collin put out his arm for her. She didn't take it at first, but he smiled and she relented with a smirk. He led her down to a royal blue Lamborghini. Samantha shot him a look he was sure she found quite effective in her classroom.

"Now don't ye go scoldin' me."

"This is your car then?"

"No, but is nay a workin' man's either. This rich man'll have it back before we're finished with it, I reckon." He opened the door for her. She slipped inside and they drove across town.

"Master O'Donnell. Welcome sir. It has been many a day since you came to see us." A well-dressed man at the door held notes and pen in his hand. "And who might your beautiful companion be this evening?"

"Samara Weiss."

"Quite fine, sir. Please come this way."

As they walked along the entrance hallway into the main ballroom, Samantha pressed herself closer to Collin. Soon they touched from knee to shoulder, sending flames of desire licking at Collin's insides. Her hands tightened around his arm until her short nails pricked his skin—through his jacket and shirt—and his fingers tingled.

The doorman passed off the note to another man in a similar uniform at the inner door. The new gentleman raised the paper and cleared his throat. "Introducing Sir Colm O'Donnell and the Lady Samara Weiss."

Collin felt Samantha tighten even more as a few heads turned. When he stepped forward he feared she wouldn't come. She fought to keep her lower lip out of her teeth. Her glaze darted about the room and her breath came in quiet puffs. Her anxious glances flittered like a manic hummingbird.

He leaned into her. "Breathe, Samantha 'tis only a party."

The color drained from her face "I am going to look like a fool and embarrass you." She turned to him. "Can't I go wait in the car? Please?"

He stepped in front of her, prying his arm free and took both her hands in his. "Ye could never embarrass me."

"Everyone's staring."

"Beauty'll do that."

Tears pooled in her eyes. "Please, I'm no good even at casual parties. There are important people here. I can't do this."

He rolled his eyes, shaking his head at her erratic behavior, but offered her soothing words. "Ye have jumped off roofs, out of trains, been smuggled on a plane, escaped bullets—this be but a wee party."

"Full of people. I'm no good with people."

Collin took her arm and led her deeper in the room. "Ye're good with me."

"You aren't people, your Col… Colm," she corrected as a man in full uniform approached them.

"General, how be ye?"

"O'Donnell, it's been a while. How is it you always manage to bring a woman more lovely than the last?" the general reached out for her hand.

"This is Samara Weiss."

"Good evening, Miss Weiss." He raised her hand to his lips and brushed it with a kiss. Samantha's cheeks flamed with color. "I am General Davidson, and should you ever wish to leave this cad, I would be most pleased to fill the void."

Samantha stifled a gasp and—though Collin

didn't think it possible—her blush deepened. She retrieved her hand and spun one of the many rings she wore about her finger, unable to speak.

By the third such encounter Samantha was nearly hyperventilating. Collin led her toward the dance floor. She stopped at the edge, tears welling once more. "Please, no. I can't."

Collin pried himself from her iron grip and stepped onto the dance floor. He raised his hand to her but remained out of her reach. "Do ye trust me?"

She trembled, her hands clasped before her until they lost their color. She then reached up to twist a strand of hair. Next she whirled the ring around her finger.

"Do ye trust me, Luv?"

Her gaze pleaded with him, but at last she reached out. He intertwined their fingers, placed her other hand on his shoulder, and encircled her waist. "Breathe, and relax." He stepped back, bringing her with him.

She followed with a jerky step. He smiled and stepped to the right. He raised her chin when she tried to look down. "Feel me movements."

She pressed into him and he moved her about the floor. She relaxed into his lead and glided with grace as one song faded into the next. Collin regretted bringing her to the dance floor, for he would never be able to dance without this moment repeating itself in his mind. But her beauty and insecurities stirred something inside of him until he could do nothing else but dance with her. He spun her across the floor knowing they would both suffer—perhaps irreparably—when they parted ways. For now—he chose to live in the bliss of this moment.

Two men approached to cut in, but Collin refused to relinquish her. If all went well, this would be their last night together. And the thought of his life after she returned home tore his heart to shreds and turned his stomach to stone. He ripped free of the coming reality. He would let her go—tomorrow.

After their fourth dance, her brows drew together. "Aren't we here for a reason?"

Collin sighed—stifling a deeper groan, "Of course. Time to get ye home."

They moved off the dance floor and Collin led her to a back corner of the room where they sat at a small round table. "Wait here—"

"Here? By myself?" She almost shrieked the words.

He patted her hand. "I'll only be a wee mite, and we can be along."

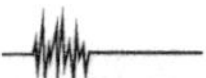

Collin slipped to the stairway and peeked up. He didn't recognize either of the guards. He moved to the hall and through the kitchen. He greeted the chief with a slap on the back and disappeared amongst the frantic staff. Peering up the rear stairs revealed one more man he also didn't know.

After a moment of calculating, he snatched a rag and lit it with the flame of the gas stove. He was stunned no one noticed him. He waited until the rag smoldered and threw it into the serving quarters at the bottom of the stairs. When the guard came to investigate Collin knocked him out, stuffed him in a closet, put out the rag, and crept up the stairs. In the library on the second floor, he removed half the books from a shelf. Behind it he tapped a panel. It dropped away, and he removed the contents hidden in the space behind. He slipped a flash drive into his inside jacket pocket and some manila files he put in his waistband behind his gun.

Collin replaced the panel and books as a familiar voice wafted through the door. He moved closer and cracked it open. Samantha teetered on the steps in front of the guards positioned at the top of the front stairs.

"You are not allowed up here," a bulky guard told her.

Samantha swayed, a near-empty martini glass in her hand. "Oh, well you're no fun," she pouted.

"Please return downstairs," the other guard said.

She shifted her gaze to look at Collin. "But there are some very unsavory characters who have arrived down there." She spun to point down below sloshing the last of the drink and tottered.

One guard grabbed her arm to steady her, the other went to collect something to clean up her mess. "Ma'am you really must return to the party."

She handed him the glass and plopped down on the top step at his feet. "Oh, I am so dizzy."

"Ma'am please."

"Don't make me go back down there. Not now. I'll ruin everything." She scanned down over the railing and leapt to her feet, nearly colliding with the guard hovering over her. She stepped back across the landing. "That man threatened me. Don't let him find me." She bolted from the guard into the room with Collin.

"How'd they find us?" Collin muttered as he led her to a window and out onto a roof.

As she teetered on the arched tiles, she held on to the window frame and removed her shoes. They inched across the roof to another lower one. Collin lifted her down and they shimmied along the wall out of the lights until they could climb down a pipe. He started down first.

"You have to be kidding me. In a dress?" she muttered at him.

He reached the ground, looked around and waved her down.

She dropped her shoes—narrowly missing him—

and pulled her skirt up between her legs, wrapping and tying it around her waist. Collin couldn't suppress the smile. She braced her bare foot against the rough wall and put one hand on the pipe. She glanced at him.

He waved her down again.

She crept toward him as Collin scanned for trouble.

A shot rang out, pinging off the pipe.

Samantha screamed.

Collin leapt forward and snatched her from the air, and they tumbled into the ivy. Once they disentangled themselves, he returned fire, grabbed Samantha's hand, and they ran. They darted across traffic and into a park. They raced between the trees and hid behind a shack-size boulder. Collin waited until one of the men stepped past their spot, leapt up and shot the man in the back of the head. Samantha covered her face and stifled a scream. Shots flashed in the dark and Collin returned fire. At least one attacker thumped to the ground.

Collin snatched up Samantha's hand, and they ran to the other side of the park, where he smoothed his hair, straightened his jacket and whistled for a passing cab. She trembled beside him as she straightened her gown. He directed the driver blocks away from their hotel.

"It's like you're Lojacked." Samantha muttered.

"What?"

She shied away from him, unwilling to repeat her revelation at first. But he persisted until she said it again so she whispered her words. "It's like you're Lojacked. You know, like someone has a GPS tracker on you."

Collin's head whipped around to look at the cabby. "Driver, head to the Pied Bull instead."

They stepped out of the cab in the parking lot of a row of white and green buildings. Collin led her a block away and stopped, ducking into the shadow. "Wait here, one mite."

Collin walked across the street to an electric company van and knocked in a very unusual rhythm on the back door. It opened with caution.

"Hello mates," Collin stepped inside.

"Who the blooming—"

"SIS, boys," he said the pass code to confirm his credentials. *Hope it's still good.* He rummaged through a few cabinets and drawers.

"What are you looking for?"

"Need an RF detector."

The nearest man jerked open a cabinet and handed him the device.

"Thanks, mate." Collin flicked it on to test the power and stepped from the van. "I'll return the favor someday."

Another taxi brought them back in the hotel. Collin prayed they had enough time to collect his pack and their dress in their street clothes before anyone caught up to them. Once inside he couldn't wait any longer and removed his suit jacket and shirt. He waved the device over his torso. It beeped around his shoulder. He handed it off to Samantha and turned around.

She passed it over him several times, but there was nothing.

He tried it again and a faint beep sputtered, tried to sound, cut off and then beeped loudly.

Samantha tried once more and it blared when it passed his right shoulder blade.

Collin cursed and stormed into the bathroom. Dragging Samantha behind him, he yanked her knife from his pack and snatched a towel from the rod. He shoved both at her hands. "Ye have to get the thin' out of me."

Samantha refused to take anything. "I'm not a surgeon."

"Ye be the only one I trust. Samantha, they'll keep comin' until we get rid of it." He sat on the toilet lid and turned his back to her. "Now, Samantha."

She placed the towel against his skin and ran her fingers over the spot. "I think I found it."

He handed her the knife. "Get rid of it."

She took it with a deep, audible breath. He

glanced at the mirror beside them, noticing her lower lip disappear between her teeth as she pressed the point against his flesh. Collin felt the bite of the blade and clenched his teeth with a groan as the cut deepened. It took her several attempts to slice deep enough to get to the bug. Once she dug it out, Collin held it in his palm. A tiny light on it fluttered from off to on to blinking. "The only reason I'm still alive is it has malfunctioned. They couldn't keep a steady bead on me." He dropped it to the floor and smashed it under his heel.

18 The Capture

Samantha wiped the blood from Collin's shoulder and pressed the towel against the wound. "We don't have anything to clean this, and the last time I used the knife was on tires." She leaned over him to snatch a washcloth from the rack over his head. She took one step toward the sink with it and his arm encircled her waist. Before she could stop him she sat in his lap.

Concern distorted his features as he grabbed for her ankle. He lifted her leg to examine her foot. "Ye're bleedin'."

"I don't recommend running across rooftops, scaling down plaster walls, or running for your life barefoot."

Collin cradled her in his arms, and carried her to the foot of one of the beds.

The sensations of his strong arms around her, and being pressed against his bare chest made her stomach do summersaults. She put her arm around his neck to secure herself—though she knew Collin would never drop her. She resisted the urge to lay her head on his shoulder.

He set her down with tender care and knelt at her feet. He took each damaged appendage in turn and wiped it with the washcloth she had intended for his wound. "Oh

Luv," he groaned.

She reached out her hand and cradled his face. "It's not your fault, Collin."

His eyes closed at her touch. He shot to his feet and slammed his fist onto the top of the low dresser. The lamp and the drawers rattled. "But it is me fault, Samantha. If not f'r me…"

She tried to stand, but he put his hand on her shoulder. "Wait here, I'll get somethin' f'r your wounds."

"And yours," she called as he snatched up his shirt and charged toward the door. He stopped in the doorway, slipped into the shirt, and froze for a moment. Retrieving the pack he pulled out a device and disappeared down the hall—leaving the door open. A moment later he returned empty handed and she again found herself snug in his arms. Collin carried her down the hall to another room with the door open and sat her on another bed. "Keep the lights low and stay quiet. I'll be back." The door closed and he was gone.

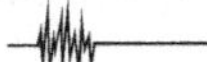

Samantha sat for another moment before she noticed the blood staining the carpet below her feet. She sighed, and wrapped the washcloth around her foot, tying it on the top. She hobbled to the bathroom for another and wrapped the other foot, before she started cleaning up their mess.

Samantha limped back to the bed and tied to find a way to sit that didn't have her getting blood everywhere. She glanced at the clock for the third time. Collin had been gone too long.

Bang!

She whirled as the door smashed open flooding the room with light from the hall. Three men—a head taller than her—stomped into the room. Samantha fell back and snatched up the lamp on the dresser. She swung it like a bat at the man closest to her.

The pottery base shattered, its jagged edges slicing the man. He bellowed and jerked back—blood dripping. The next attacker took his place as she brought the broken weapon back across the space between them. The rough edge cut deep into his cheek and his hand, spraying the wall with blood. He too fell away, and the last approached her.

The man's narrow, dark gaze locked on her, sending a frigid wave coursing down her spine. He knocked the weapon from her hand and took a swing at her. She ducked under his attack and scrambled to get on the bed—regretting she still wore the floor length dress.

The three men lurched toward her. She kicked and lashed out at them, but her efforts were no match against three trained assailants. One snatched her from the bed, slammed her down on the floor with such force her knees shuddered.

He grasped her arms. She whooped as she slipped free, her satin dress having the same effect as trying to catch a greased pig. She kneed the man in front of her, doubling him over, and spun from the grasp of the one behind her. Now facing him, she put her lesson from Collin into practice. Samantha balled up her fist—thumb on the outside—and drove it at the man's face. She succeeded in connecting with his nose. She smiled at the satisfying snap and the view of blood covering the mirror beside him.

A hand pounded on her shoulder and spun her around. The back of a hand crashed into her cheek, sending her flying—

Collin cursed himself for not allowing Samantha to remain behind as she'd requested. Seeing her shredded feet heaped an unbearable weight of guilt on top of the load he already carried. He further chastised himself, for the nearest open pharmacy ended up being miles away. He returned to their room, lumbering up the stairs with heavy feet. His hand ran over his neck in rough waves and he grabbed the aching muscle and squeezed. Could he face her? Surely she tired of this life—and him—by now.

Collin glanced at his watch. Ninety minutes. His

errand took too long. He quickened his pace—up the stairs. The motel sat almost vacant and he had requested a room far from anyone else. He rounded the corner. Her door stood ajar, and his stomach rolled in nauseous waves while air fled from his lungs.

He dropped the purchases on the floor in the hall. Drawing his gun, he pushed open the door with caution. Something lay in his path. He flipped on the light and saw a broken, blood-covered lamp lay discarded on the floor. Blood castoff showered most of the walls, and a red pool stained the carpet next to the dresser. He ran down the hall to their first room. The door had been kicked in there, too. Samantha was gone.

Returning to the blood-covered room, Collin staggered back, bumping into the door behind him, shutting it. His lungs turned to stone and his gun dropped to the floor. Trembling legs carried him forward a few steps, but gave way and he fell to his knees. Hot tears of fear and anger burned his face.

An unknown time passed in the abyss of his despair. Collin became aware of something soft under his right knee. He reached under the bed and withdrew the packs.

Logic and reason bolted across his brain like gunfire. He found and assembled the phone as he moved to sit on the bed. The beeps of the number being entered quickened his pulse.

"Hello, United Health Care. How may I direct your call?"

"Code Blizzard," Collin barked. "Agent eight, seven, two, five, seven, six, one, five. Password, Rambler."

"I'm sorry, sir. I'm afraid you have the wrong—"

"Be givin' me Declan Mason now! I don't care how old me security words be. Give me Declan!"

"Sir, there is no reason to yell—"

"A woman's life—a fabulous woman's—life is at stake. Be connectin' me to Declan now or I'll be stormin' headquarters with me guns ablaze."

Click. Hum.

"Collin?" a tentative voice called.

"Mase. I know I've screwed up. I'll do it. I'll kill whoever ye want. The leader of Andorra and his whole family, the president of Russia—the queen herself. But let Samantha go."

"Collin, what are you talking about?"

"I'll do the job Mase. I'll come in out of the cold. Ye can torture me or kill me. Please, ye have to let Samantha go."

"Collin you went rogue eighteen months ago."

Collin shot to his feet. *Eighteen months—that wasn't right.* He paced to the interior wall shaking his head. "Nay, it hasn't been so long. I but refused the Andorra job a month ago."

"What Andorra job? Collin we've had no contact with you or Elsa or any of her team for eighteen months. I know nothing about any trouble in Andorra—but if there is a hit planned on their prime minister and his family that could certainly lead to huge complications in the area."

Collin raked his fingers over his hair. Mutters filtered over the line. Declan couldn't allow a threat to go unanswered. He'd task someone with looking into it before he returned to the conversation. Collin continued on his circuit across the room trying to calculate back over the months. *Eighteen months? What was I doin' then. Eighteen months...* "The kid!"

"What? Oh right, Collin. Yes, the ambassador's son died eighteen months ago. I figured Elsa used the incident to convince you to turn dark."

"I haven't turned dark!" Collin shouted. "I messed up. The boy died. Elsa hid me away—told me ye said no communication until it blew over. The next thin'..."

"We did a full investigation. Someone kidnapped the boy, and took him to the side of town where you planted the charge a day before your strike. He escaped moments before you hit the trigger and they chased him right into the line of the blast." Declan reported with directness.

Collin dropped back to the bed. Thoughts shot across his mind like a crazed machine gun—hitting everything but a clear target.

"You are not responsible for his death, Collin." Declan sighed. "Unfortunately, you never called so I couldn't tell you the truth. You have been disavowed. Whatever trouble you are in now, is beyond my aid."

"Mase, please. I didn't go rogue."

"You've been with Elsa all this time—"

"But I didn't know she wasn't with ye!" Collin's shouts rattled the windows. "Mase, listen. Ye know me. I wouldn't be leavin'—not like this. Mase, an innocent woman be caught up in it now. An American. Elsa called a hit on me f'r refusin' the Andorra job. Samantha got caught in the crossfire. Russians, Columbians, and who knows who else been chasing me across three continents. Now they have Samantha. Mase I'll do anythin'. I'll hunt down Elsa and her entire network. I'll kill 'm all. But ye have to be helpin' me get Samantha back."

A long sigh answered him. "I believe you, Collin, but the regulations—"

Collin cursed. "Forget the bloomin' regs. Be gettin' me Samantha and I be yers. Do with me as ye please."

"Give me an hour."

19 The End

Like a gasping fish on the shore is revived by a wave, a cascade of water jolted Samantha back to consciousness. The torrent burned a spot on her head. Had she been knocked out? The water continued downward, stinging her eyes, and biting at her cracked lips. Awareness dawned. Pain shot through her arms. Her head throbbed. She inwardly begged for oblivion to return. She blinked away the tears and licked at her lips, tasting salt. She raised her head between her arms. She hung suspended by handcuffs on a hook, whose chain disappeared into the dark above. The handcuffs tore into the flesh at the base of her thumbs and the backs of her hands. Blood slid down her arms, making dark ripples along her sleeves.

She dangled with the tips of her toes brushing over an odd depression in the cement floor—the water pooled almost ankle deep. A spotlight on a tripod shone in her face, but cavernous black filled everything else. A door banged shut and echoed in the empty space. She shuddered.

As the man who dumped the salt-water on her slipped into the shadows with this bucket, a man dressed in black slacks and a shiny black button-up shirt materialized out of the surrounding darkness. His dark hair clung slicked-back and oily-looking to his bowling ball-shaped head. His smile—more a sneer—sent another shiver through her.

"So de sleeping beauty wakes?" The strong accented words reverberated off distant unseen walls, though for the life of her, Samantha could figure out where the man might be from.

She clamped her lips closed and held his gaze. She'd never be called a beauty, and the sting of his mocking—as she hung dripping wet, battered, and bruised—bit like a viper.

"Where is he?"

"Who?" Samantha quipped.

The man pinched her chin between his thumb and first knuckle and spoke in her face. The liquor vapors spun in her head. She wrinkled her nose at the fumes. "You will not want to be playing games with me, chick-a-dee." He leaned even closer—still holding her face—and whispered in her ear, "Little dove, you will not fly from my snare."

Samantha tipped her head back, freeing herself from his grasp.

He backed a step and glared.

"I would never play games with you, Sir. I know I would lose such a contest."

He nodded once. "So I ask again, dove, where is he?"

"You still have not told me the name of the man you wish to find." Everything in her vibrated with an uncontrollable fear, but the words wouldn't remain silent on her tongue. It wagged and jabbered of its own volition. She swallowed hard in a vain effort to keep any more from bursting forth. "Who plays the games now?" *Lord, send Collin. No. Better—save him.*

He roared. His arms flew at her. One behemoth hand seized her by the hair the other slapped her face.

Tears pooled in her eyes, but refused to escape and betray her. She couldn't tell which lasted longer—the slap's repeating echo or the waves of pain lapping her skin.

"Collin Fitzpatrick!" He shook her. "Where is Collin Fitzpatrick?"

"I don't know."

He pushed her away, sending her swinging—her toes scraped the concrete and the cuffs cut deeper into her hands. "Have it your way, little dove!"

He waved another man from the shadows. Dressed in jeans and dark polo, he carried a rusty chair. On it sat a black cube. It wasn't until he connected the cables to the cube that it dawned on her what he carried.

Samantha fought to control the fear clawing

inside her.

Greasy Hair stepped toward her, waving a long knife like the one she used on the get-away car. He brought the tip to her chin. "Where is he?"

She said each word with slow purpose. "I—do—not—know."

Greasy Hair growled.

Samantha squeezed her eyes shut and held her ragged breath.

He used the knife to slit the front of her dress to the waist, and muttered something unintelligible.

Samantha opened her eyes to see Polo Shirt approach. Battery cables sparked. He touched them to her skin.

Collin sat in another "borrowed" vehicle. Samantha would be cross with him—and the fact added to his grief. As his watch ticked off the last of the hour Mase requested, Collin dropped the battery back into his phone and powered it on. It rang the instant it connected to the network.

"Hello—"

"There you are Collin," Mase gasped. "Man, if you want my help, you've got to keep your phone on."

"What'd ye—"

"Surveillance shows a woman in a red dress being carried from the location you last called—around eleven twenty."

"Samantha. How'd she look?"

"She appeared unconscious, slung over an assailant's shoulder."

Collin groaned and his head hung. He pressed his thumb and finger against his temples.

"They put her in one of a few vehicles, and we tracked them..."

Collin turned the key of the Astra, and threw it into gear.

"...to the warehouse district near Walthamstow...

Tires squealed as Collin sped off.

"...The old plant off Argall Avenue and Staffa Road appears deserted, but satellite shows several cars there and movement around the property."

"Got it Mase." Collin moved to disconnect.

"Collin, I can't send any assistance."

"Not asking f'r any. No skin off me nose if ye be wantin' foreign thugs runnin' amuck in the country."

"You know that's not true. Officially, I don't know who is out there. I can't very well say we have surveillance of her majesty's citizens and we know there are some terrorists—"

"Ye be a smart man, Mase. I'm sure ye could be

comin' up with somethin'."

"You have always been the most impatient fool." Mase growled. "What I've been trying to tell you is, I'll give you time to get there, and I'll call Scotland Yard to report suspicious activity at the rear of the Bates Laundry plant."

"Thanks," Collin muttered.

"Go get your girl, Collin. And be safe, my friend."

Collin tossed the phone into the passenger seat. Mase knew his destination. If he wanted to set a trap to catch him, Samantha would die. He weaved through light traffic, trying not to draw the attention of the bobbies. But fear pushed him faster.

A siren blared. He cursed and hit the stirring wheel with his fist. *Pull over f'r the ticket and risk the car had already been reported stolen—or speed away.* One in the morning in London provided clearer streets, but there was always some traffic. The cop car closed the distance as Collin slowed in indecision. He moved toward the curb as Samantha's screams filled his thoughts.

Samantha's muscles constricted violently as the electricity from the car battery roared through her salt-water covered body. Bones snapped. Her teeth clamped shut, nipping her tongue. Metal flavored her mouth. Burnt flesh filled her nostrils. Pain overwhelmed her.

Then nothing.

She hung limp. Her muscles twitched. Her heart skittered about in her chest with wild uncontrolled rhythm. She struggled to draw an even breath. Logic told her the connectors only touched her for moments—though it felt like a lifetime. But fear told her she could never last long under this torture.

Greasy Hair stepped forward lifting her chin. "Where is he?"

Tears escaped. "I don't know."

He waved for Polo Shirt to return.

"You can continue until I die, but I will never know where Mr. Fitzpatrick is. He left me. I am a civilian —"

The electrodes touched her again. Her head flung back between her arms, and an anguished scream squeezed through her locked jaw.

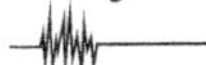

Greasy Hair slapped her face to wake her. "Tell me where he is and it will stop."

"I don't know!" she screamed with the weak puff of breath she could expel from her aching lungs. "He tired of me. I weighed him down—slowed his progress— hampered his escape."

The cables touched her again.

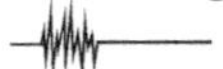

Samantha opened her eyes to the red and black burned welts on her flesh. She fought for an even breath as her lungs and heart fought in competing rhythms.

"End this while you may, dove."

"Collin left the hotel room," she gasped. "Under the guise of getting first aid for my wounds. He had been gone an hour..."

Pops sounded in the distance, drawing Greasy Hair's attention away. He waved Polo Shirt to stay and continue as he melted into the blackness. The echo of a large metal door sliding open filled the cavernous space. Light from outside the door flooded the left side of the room.

The light shone off large metal machinery, reminding her of huge washing machines as the electrodes assaulted her once more.

Collin waited until the officer stopped next to the curb behind him and had walked half the distance to his door before stomping on the gas pedal and speeding away. He wasted time hiding in unlit alleys as more officers searched. It was taking him too long to evade them.

After nearly another hour, no bobbies passed, or

appeared in his path. He turned his car toward the plant only to ditch it a block away. From the trunk, he collected the assault weapons he'd retrieved while waiting for Mase, and crept to a place of good vantage.

With a scope on the long-range rifle, he picked off two perimeter guards. He moved through the shadows, collected their weapons, and hid the bodies. With their weapons added to those already slung across his chest, he came up behind another guardand seized him around the neck. The man got off a few shots before Collin snapped his neck.

Shouts and gunfire filled the air.

Collin dove for cover and returned fire. If he didn't get them all quickly, Samantha would die. *Hang on, Luv. I'm on me way.*

The pops were closer. She raised her head and opened her eyes, though they didn't stay open for long. *Gunfire?* Her mind couldn't reason. *Collin? How could he have found me?* She raised her head in hope, but her heart stuttered in fear. *No, don't come. They'll kill you. Save yourself. Lord, don't let him die for me. Please.*

Polo Shirt stepped toward her again.

The pops and pings were inside the building— growing closer. Unintelligible shouts added to the cacophony.

Polo Shirt turned his back on her.

Samantha summoned the last ounce of her strength, twisted her right wrist and gripped the chain of the cuff holding her. Her left wrist would not respond because it was one of the first bones that broke, and it throbbed now with unbearable pain.

She lifted her legs up and looped her right leg around her attacker's neck—like Collin did to her in her house. She caught the top of her right foot with the calf of her left leg and squeezed.

He brought the cables up to her leg, but the electricity ran through them both. She squeezed his neck tighter.

She held him fast.

Holding the cables apart, he beat against her shin with his forearms.

She ignored the pain and held.

He gasped and writhed.

She kept him in her grip.

His arms slid down at his sides and he grew heavy. He dropped limp to the floor, falling in the puddle. Electricity sparked, sending his body twitching and thrashing.

Samantha held her feet above him to keep from being electrocuted too.

The sparks slowed and the body stilled.

She put her feet down and stood on the dead man, taking the weight off her arms. Her heart beat an erratic rhythm. She lowered her body until she hung once more.

Gunfire erupted outside as her head sagged and she let go of a long breath—releasing herself into oblivion. *Lord, I'm Yours. Save Collin.*

Collin fired a volley, killing the last two men outside, and moved to the entrance. He flung the door open, but remained out of sight. A few shots welcomed him. He determined the direction and entered, guns spewing a hail of bullets. He leapt behind a fallen desk and waited for his eyes to adjust to the light.

Gunfire came from multiple directions, followed by shouts in Croatian from a voice he recognized.

"Roko, be lettin' the woman go, and we can be discussin' this as men."

A harsh laugh answered. "She's served her purpose. I have no further need of her." Roko shouted in Croatian. "Kill her."

Collin sprang from safety, showering the room with bullets. When his weapon ran out, he dropped it and drew another from his shoulder. He moved forward on the men, knowing, whether he lived or died, the only way to assure Samantha's safety would be if he killed them all.

The enemy fell one after the other. Collin took a bullet to the left shoulder as he threw down another empty weapon. Three more fell as he chased down Roko and a handful of his men. He followed them down a hall with no protection for either of them as they shot at one another from doorways.

"Be givin' her up, Roko, and I'll be lettin' ye live."

A curse answered him, and two more of his smuggler's men fell.

Those with Roko expended the last of their bullets and Collin advanced unhampered. He shot each one in turn as he approached. Stepping over bodies, he pursued the last few. He dropped Roko as the man tried to jerk open a sliding door.

Collin peered into the room. His rifle clattered to the ground with an echo. He shoved the door open and staggered into the dark space. Samantha hung bathed in light—but lifeless. A body lay limp at her feet.

Collin choked back tears. "Good f'r ye, Luv. Ye took one of them with ye." He crumbled back into the wall under the guilt crushing him. Logic, reason, and clear thought fled. Convinced he'd failed her like he had Katie, he moaned, "I be so sorry. I let ye down, Luv. Forgive me." He reached for the handgun at the small of his back and raised it to his temple. "Accept her spirit, God. She was a fine woman and deserved better than the likes of me." His finger moved to the trigger.

20 The Rescue

The gun dropped to Collin's side, unfired, as his
head hung low. He pushed himself off the wall and
dragged himself toward Samantha. "I can't leave ye like
this—exposed and battered. I'll keep me promise to see ye
home, Luv. I owe ye as much."

His arm trembled as he reached out to encircle her
waist to lift her off the hook.

The muscles of her stomach rippled at his tender
touch. Her flesh still felt warm. His hand continued
around her back. Her head looked like it moved. Collin's
heart slammed to a stop, then burst into erratic pounding.
He tightened his grip around her waist.

A whimper slipped from her still lips.

He laid his ear on her breast and thrilled at the
uneven rhythm of her heart. "Samantha? Thank the
Almighty!" He lifted her to ease the pressure of the cuffs
and reached up with his other hand to release her from the
hook.

She crumpled into his arms with a moan. He laid
her on the floor away from the water, unbuttoned his shirt,
and he slipped it off. Raising her up, he worked it on her.
No more whimpers or groans escaped her, and Collin felt
for her heartbeat once more.

"I have ye Luv. Ye're safe. Don't ye be givin' up on me now."

Sirens sounded in the distance as Collin scooped her up in his arms and ran for the nearest vehicle, thanking the Almighty again that the keys were in it. He sped away in the opposite direction of the arriving law enforcement.

"Hello?" a voice called as bare feet descended the stairs. A light flicked on, and the man staggered back from the woman's body lying across his kitchen table. "What the blooming—"

Collin looked up at the army medic from his unit. "I be needin' yer help, Bailey."

"Fitzpatrick! You nearly scared me to death."

"She's hurt bad."

"You've been disavowed, you know." He turned toward the phone. "I'm supposed to—"

Collin placed a gun at his temple. "Ye be me mate, Bay. I be wishin' ye no harm, but if ye be needin' the deniability of bein' forced to render aid at gun point, I can be obligin' ye."

Bailey raised his hands in surrender and turned back to his patient. "What did you do to her?"

"She got mixed up in this by no fault of her own. Roko caught her and tortured her to get to me." Collin lifted his shirt she wore to reveal the electrical burns.

Grabbing a medical bag from a nearby cabinet, Bailey slipped a stethoscope into his ears and put it to her heart. "The shocks have caused an irregular heartbeat. If it isn't corrected she will die.

Collin waved the gun at him to continue.

"I don't have a defibrillator in my house, Fitzpatrick. You have to take her to the hospital."

"I can't. They'll be getting' her again—or kill her outright."

"I could take her."

"No. They already be knowin' who she is now. Elsa has spoken to her on the phone. She won't be safe."

Bailey moved to the phone again. He pushed away the gun butt. "You have to trust me if you want her to live."

"Freya? Yes, I realize it is three thirty in the morning. I have a unique emergency, and I need you to go open the clinic—no questions asked. I owe you, thanks." Bailey hung up the phone and picked up car keys from the bowl on the same table. Handing them to Collin, he said, "Dr. Freya Ryan will meet you at the medical centre at 999 Finchly Road. Hurry, your girlfriend doesn't have much time."

Collin kicked at the medical centre door with his

foot. Samantha lay limp in his arms. The lock clicked, and the door pushed open. A middle-aged woman with bags under her eyes and disheveled hair motioned for him to follow her to an exam room. Collin laid Samantha on the table.

"Bailey says she needs a defibrillator."

The doctor removed her stethoscope from around her neck and listened for a moment. She turned and retrieved a small box from a drawer. She opened the shirt and placed the contacts on Samantha's exposed skin.

Collin diverted his gaze and stared at the beeping monitor.

"Stand clear," the doctor instructed.

Collin stepped away.

The doctor's right brow hitched high and her glance dropped to Collin's hand clasping Samantha's. He placed her hand on the table, heat filling his cheeks.

The doctor pressed the button. Samantha's back rose off the exam table, and she whimpered again. She sagged down, and the machine beeped in a consistent cadence.

"Now we have the most urgent dealt with, let's see what else I can do for her—and you." She pointed to his bleeding shoulder. "May I ask a name?"

"Samantha."

The doctor spent the next two hours examining

and treating Samantha's many injuries. She glanced up at
the clock. "I've done as much as I can here." She handed
him a paper bag. "This is all the medicine, ointment, and
bandages I can spare for her. Keep those wounds clean,
but she would be best in a hospital. If her temperature
spikes, infection has set in and you'll have no other
choice."

The bell on the front door jingled.

"Come on with you. My partner has arrived.
You'll have to go out the back."

Collin slipped out without even time for a
muttered thanks as Dr. Ryan closed the door on him. He
carried Samantha around the building and down an alley
toward Bailey's small car. He placed her inside and
headed out of town.

They both slept in the car as the ferry carried
them across the channel. Once on the mainland, Collin
spent several days driving across various countries to a
secluded cabin nestled at the foot of the Alps while
Samantha slept in the backseat. Now, days later, Samantha
lay as still as when he found her. She never really woke.
Though in the first day she tossed and turned in pain and
fear.

Collin touched her forehead for the millionth
time. Radiating heat seared his hand. He moved across the

room toward the fireplace and assembled yet another burner phone.

"Mase, I need yer help again."

"Collin, are you all right? Where are you?"

"Ye'll be havin' a trace soon enough. She is in a bad way, Mase. Ye have to be getting' her and see to it she receives proper treatment. But Mase, ye have to swear to me she'll be safe."

"Collin, you can both come in and we'll get the whole mess straightened out."

"Mase, be swearin' it on the lives of yer children, and I'll do whatever ye want. I kill all ye want killin'."

"I promise you, Collin, no further harm will come to her."

"Swear it!"

"I swear it, on the lives of my children—your godchildren—no harm will come to Samantha. I promise you, I will see her home safe."

Collin exhaled a sigh as a gust of cold air brushed his cheek.

He turned to see the front door open. His gaze flew to the bed. Empty. He dropped the phone with a shout of Samantha's name.

He followed her bare footprints in the snow about a yard from the cabin and found her face down. "Samantha!" He scooped her up and raced back inside, set her by the fire, and yanked the blankets from the bed. "By all that be holy, what were you thinkin', Luv?"

As Collin cradled her and rubbed her warm, Samantha's eyes fluttered. Through chattering teeth, she muttered, "Not for me, don't return to Elsa for me."

Collin held her close, muttering, "What happened to no martyrs?"

She didn't reply as she drifted off once more.

He picked up the phone. "Mase, ye still there?"

"Yes, and a chopper will arrive in about an hour. You can come in Collin—"

"Not until I've repaid Elsa for the pain she caused Samantha." He swished the connection off but left the phone on. He moved Samantha to the bed, and prepared himself.

Forty-five minutes later, Collin hovered over her, his hand cradling her face. "Luv, ye've been the best thin' to ever happen to me. I be sorry for all the pain I've caused." He swiped at a tear. "Mase be a friend and will be keepin' ye safe now. I know he'll be doin' a much better job. Ye go home and have a great life now, ye hear me?"

A whispered moan slid between her lips, and she pressed her cheek into his hand.

Collin swiped at another tear, and moved to the door. "I shall miss ye, Luv." he stepped out into a cold wind, raised the hood on a heavy coat, and moved toward the tree line. A few minutes later, he watched as a helicopter came to rest in the clearing behind the cabin. He stayed until they lifted off and disappeared across the valley.

Now it be high time f'r ye to be payin' f'r yer crimes, Elsa. I be comin' f'r ye.

21 The Recovery

Beep, beep, beep. Samantha wanted to swat the annoying sound away like some hovering insect. She drifted in a world without substance, like an anchorless boat on the sea. A smell joined the sound—familiar, yet she couldn't name it. A couple of her limbs felt heavy and bound, while the others complained with a dull ache. She floated again.

The beeps grew louder, the smell more pungent, the pain radiated throughout her body. *Where am I?* All her memories lurked on the edge of her awareness just out of reach—a dense fog at the edge of her sea.

She battled to open her eyes, move, speak, scream —anything. Her body wouldn't respond. Cold sweat added to her discomfort. Bits of memory flashed like a defective DVD, and her heart pounded. *Why am I afraid?* Voices from her memories drifted to her in incoherent jumbles. Her heart raced until she thought it might explode. The beeping increased.

A hand grabbed her wrist.

Samantha's mind lurched like a revving car thrown into gear.

Collin—running—jumping—trains—bullets— jumper cables—pain. It all hit her at once with the speed of a runaway locomotive. She jerked free with a yelp as her eyes flew open.

The slight woman standing next to her bed gasped. "Oh, dearie! You gave me a fright, child."

The lilt of her British accent fell soft on Samantha's ears. She jerked her hands out of reach and clutched them to her chest.

"You are safe now, Miss Wellington. No one here will harm you."

Though a kind smile graced her face, Samantha couldn't control the pounding of her heart, which the beeping monitor beside the bed announced to everyone within one hundred feet of her room. *Hospital? How did I get here? Where is Collin?* Her mind wandered back to the warehouse—hanging from the ceiling, (she noted the bandage on her right wrist and the cast on her left.). *What happened there?* The last memories came slow like a tiger creeping through the jungle.

Hanging—torture! *I was tortured—by...by...a man with an accent and greasy hair?* He left, another stayed. *I killed him. I killed the man who placed battery cables...* She shuddered.

"Truly dear, you're safe," the nurse reached out a hand toward her arm, but Samantha cringed and shied away.

Bursts of pain accompanied her movements.

The nurse clicked her tongue. "Perhaps a spot of food will help. You must be quite famished."

The nurse left the room while Samantha fought for any memory after the warehouse. The vague images of a car, water, and snow teased her but would not reveal their secrets. The efforts to bring up the memories tired her, and she released her spirit to the boat adrift in the waves, surrounded by fog.

Samantha rolled her shoulders. *Pop. Snap.* A yawn stretched her mouth wide and she let it seep out in a long lazy breath. One brow rose, tugging on her lid. Blurry shapes congealed. A man sat beside her bed. Samantha opened both eyes and stared at him. Distinguished in his grey suit and dark tie, his neatly trimmed hair sparkled with a few grey highlights. He sat straighter when she stirred, and his head tipped to one side as his gaze focused on her.

He rubbed his chin for a moment, and his soft tone held an air of wonder. "Hello Miss Wellington, I am much relieved to see you are recovering." His voice caressed the air like a balm. "My name is Declan Mason. Collin calls me Mase."

The infuriating heart monitor betrayed her again as her pulse quickened at the mere mention of Collin's name.

"You made quite an impression on him, Miss Willington. I've known Collin for many years and never have I seen his head so flummoxed."

Samantha's heart beat harder.

Mr. Mason slid to the end of his seat. "I am the director of SIS. Can you tell me what happened?"

Her heart pounded near out of her chest, until the rush of blood through her ears drowned out the mechanical beeping. Elsa's smooth lies sprang to mind. She talked of Collin too, spinning tales about him to her own twisted end. Elsa lied and Samantha almost lost her trust of Collin. *Not again.* Who was this man really? Where was Collin? She turned her head away and closed her eyes. Let him try and get anything from her. Perhaps he would get lucky, and she might talk in her sleep. A smirk twisted her lips as Collin's words tickled her memory. *Not bloomin' likely.*

Mr. Mason sighed, and the click of his shoes faded from the room.

But he returned each day to sit beside her bed, assured her she was safe, and asked her about Collin. On the fourth day, he beamed as he entered her room. He held a tablet out to her.

Samantha took it and in a moment Collin's face materialized on the screen. She rejoiced at the blessed silence now that the monitor no longer reported how her heart thrilled to see him.

"Hello, Luv," his crooked smile drew up the corners of her own lips. "Ye be well?"

She couldn't find the words to speak but gave him an eager nod of her head.

He rubbed his neck and his lips drew in a line. He blinked several times as his gaze tried to avoid her one moment but struggled to look away the next. He wet his lips. "I am powerful sorry, Luv. I never—"

"It's not your fault. I'm fine, truly. But, what about you? Are you safe?"

His image trembled, but his full smile returned at last. He nodded his head. "Aye, I'm well, now I see ye be safe, and hear ye be mendin'." He looked at her for a moment as if studying her face. "Mase asked me to contact ye. I appreciate more than ye know wantin' to keep me safe, Luv. But Mase speaks the truth. He be me boss, and ye can be trustin' him. Tell him whatever he be wantin' to know."

Samantha cocked her head and considered him.

He smirked, nodded, and turned the device he held away from his face to take in his surroundings. "See, I be free as a bird. No one be holdin' me against me will."

"Where are you?"

His face again filled the screen and Samantha's heart fluttered once more. "I be chasin' down Elsa's gang and bringin' them to justice."

Samantha searched his face, not daring to ask the questions beating against the back of her teeth.

"I won't be seein' ye again, Luv. I'll stay clear of ye. I've done enough harm. Ye return home and live a good life, Samantha Wellington."

The screen went black.

She sank back against the bed and fought for breath. Her heart plummeted to her stomach, causing it to churn and heave. She put her hand over her mouth, sweat beading on her face. So she'd been right, wasn't worth fighting for after all. She tossed her head and swallowed her tears. *He's better off.*

Mr. Mason stepped forward again and reached for the tablet. "Are you willing to talk to me now, Miss Wellington?"

She blinked back the last of the unshed tears and nodded. "What would you like to know?"

Samantha's fingers drummed on her bed rail as Mr. Mason entered. She'd lost track of how many days he darkened her room. Did he expect her to change her story? Maybe he thought asking the same questions ad nauseam would jog her memory into revealing something new. She knew nothing of value. Her head dropped back against her pillow and she threw up her hands. They flopped beside her as her teeth ground together, adding to the ache in her head.

He asked his familiar questions. She gave the answers that were now mindless rote words with no meaning. And Mr. Mason left again.

Day in and day out, it was always the same.

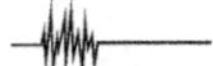

A check of the time and a slow breath eased from her, as she glanced heavenward. Mr. Mason remained absent today. Perhaps he was at last done with her. She shifted, settling back into the mound of pillows and reached for the remote. A flash of light filled the screen, followed slowly by the image and finally the sound. Formal British dialog and canned laughter made her press the channel button in search of something else.

Nothing interesting on the *'bloomin' telly'*. She clicked it off and moved out of bed. Still a little sore and achy in places, she took her time to slide each arm into the thin cotton robe. Hanging onto the bed, she slid one foot into backless sleepers and shuffled toward the door, the other foot was bound up in a walking boot.

Mr. Mason appeared in the doorway.

She stumbled back, gasped, and clutched at the IV pole to steady herself as her other hand flew to her chest.

He offered his arm and waited for her to collect herself again.

One hand on her IV pole, the other looped in his arm, she hobbled, on legs stiff from disuse, down the quiet hall and back. "I don't remember anything new today, Mr. Mason. I would tell you if I did."

"I know Miss Wellington. I came merely to check your welfare."

"I'm little changed from yesterday. I've been here for nearly a month—by my best calculation. It's a bit hard to keep track of the days in this windowless ward."

He nodded, but stared straight ahead. "You are safe here. This may be the safest place you can be at this time."

"I thought Collin took care of all the men who tortured me and with a month separating our contact I would be of no value to anyone now."

Mr. Mason chuckled.

Samantha cocked a brow at him, for his 'stiff upper lip' British attitude did not seem to lend itself to chuckling.

"You have failed to take one thing into account, my dear."

"And what would that be, sir?"

"The feelings Collin harbors for you."

Samantha stopped walking, her hand squeezed tighter on his arm, and she stared at him. "What feelings?"

He glanced at her, and his amusement danced on

his lips. "The man loves you, my dear."

Her knees went weak.

Mason wrapped a steadying hand around her and led her to a bench along the wall. "This can't come as a surprise to you, Miss Wellington."

She fought for breath and couldn't answer.

Mr. Mason patted her hand and waited.

"I…" She tipped back her head, taking a deep breath while closing her eyes. "He left me. I thought…"

"He left because he cares too much to see you get caught up in his troubles again. It would kill him if anything happened to you. This is why you are still here. He won't allow us to release you to be taken and used to get to him."

"You really think he cares for me?" She searched his face, unable to wrap her befuddled thoughts around the unbelievable notion.

"Of this, Miss Wellington, I have no doubt."

"Collin loves me," she sighed more to herself than to Mr. Mason.

"Yes he does, my dear. But I fear he will never act on those feelings. As I said he would never forgive himself if anything happened to you because of him. He even told you himself, he would never see you again."

Mr. Mason's brows drew together as he considered her with an unwavering gaze.

"There is something we must discuss. Miss Wellington. Have you given any thought to what you will tell people upon your return to your life in the States?"

She stared off at the nurses as they came and went from the various rooms. Her ankles crossed. "I have, Mr. Mason." She let her mind wander, bringing her old life to the forefront of her thoughts. Her vision blurred until images appeared of her coworkers milling about the school office, as the excuse for why she had been missing for months spilled over her lips. "It was all a huge misunderstanding. A group of people thought I was someone else—ended up being a case of stolen identity. I had to go here, there and everywhere to get the whole mess straightened out. It has to be the biggest headache ever. It is amazing how easy it is to convince people you are someone other than who you are—but near impossible to prove you are—you."

"Who stole your identity?"

She shrugged, still not seeing him but hearing old familiar voices. "I have no idea. The authorities have a man trying to chase down the culprits now."

"But you were gone forever."

"Apparently the other me bolted from one city to another all over the country in a continuous crime wave, wreaking havoc everywhere she went. There were quite a lot of warrants out for me and I had to deal with each one in turn." She groaned and her shoulders sagged. "It has been a huge pain in my backside."

"Was that your house that got shot up?"

"A bunch of my neighbors and I had our windows shot out—some gang drive-by thing. Happened about the same time all this other mess came to light."

His hand rested on her forearm, drawing her from her imagined explanations. A gentle smile welcomed her back. "It sounds plausible enough. We can put some trails in the records to confirm your tale if anyone should search out the details. But do you think it will be enough to convince your friends and family?"

"I've never had reason to lie to anyone, Mr. Mason. They'll be inclined to accept whatever I tell them. But more than that, I know if they ever discover the truth, they'll be in danger. Anything they find out could put Collin at risk too. I'll not allow anyone else to get sucked into this with me. I'll make sure they believe me."

He sat back, his shoulders relaxed. He nodded at her for a moment. "Yes, Miss Wellington, I am sure you will. If a trained assassin couldn't break you, I doubt a bunch of teachers could."

She tipped her chin up, and threw back her shoulders. "Indeed. I have been weighed, I have been measured, and I have *not* been found wanting."

"Of that, I never had a doubt. As I told you, I've

known Collin for a long time and he would never become infatuated with a woman of less than trustworthy character." He rose, led her back to her room, and left her to waste away her day watching British television. She needed a *Dr. Who* marathon.

22 The Letter

Collin loved her—but he had no intention of ever
seeing her again. Her head spun, stirring her stomach into
uncomfortable rolls. Mr. Mason also expected the excuse
she devised to fool all her coworkers and friends. He
believed it enough to plant a trail—not that anyone she
knew would ever check up on her wild story. She really
did pray everyone would believe her. She couldn't risk
Collin…*Oh Collin, what are we going to do?*

*No man has ever loved me. Surely this is not what
was intended. We have been brought together for some
reason from worlds so far apart they never should have
crossed.*

She paced up and down the hall. She moved with
less pain and the cast on her arm had been replaced with a
brace a couple of days earlier. *We're meant to be together
—I know it. I'll continue to trust you, Collin, and wait—as
long as it takes.*

More than a week passed before Mr. Mason
visited again. He arrived holding a shopping bag in one
hand and an envelope in the other. He looked at her with a
drawn face and a small nod. "Well, I know you wish to
return home. The doctors report you are all but healed

from your injuries. The walking boot should no longer be needed in another couple of weeks. And you have been cleared to return home."

He offered the shopping bag to her. "These are for you. I hope everything fits." His cheeks flushed. "I make no claims to their fashionable rightness, but my assistant Zoe picked them out and I have never known her to be frumpy or unkempt."

Samantha couldn't suppress a bubble of laughter at his discomfort. "I am sure whatever is in this bag will be far better than a hospital gown and robe, Mr. Mason. Thank you." She took the bag from him, and he inclined his head, escaping from the room.

She dressed in the jeans and slipped on the long sleeved blouse of muted colors. She plopped into a chair to slip on the sock and lace up the one tennis shoe she could wear. She put her hands in the back pockets, doing a little spin to see the fit from all angles. A sigh passed her smiling lips. She snatched up the jacket and bounded into the hall to meet Mr. Mason.

He did a quick glance before meeting her gaze. "Well, that doesn't appear so terrible."

"It is marvelous, Mr. Mason. Please thank Zoe for me. I feel a thousand times better."

"Well, I will admit, I will be sorry to see you go, Miss Wellington." He turned from her. "The lift is this way." Once they stepped inside he pointed to an envelope. "You will find a little cash, and plane tickets home."

He pushed the button for the ground floor and she watched the five floors click off as they rose to their destinations, confirming Samantha's suspicion. She had convalesced hidden away in a secret basement area of a medical facility. The doors whooshed open to a hospital admittance area. He led the way out to the street where a black sedan waited.

He opened the back door for her. "Mr. Atwood will take you to the airport. Cheerio, Miss Wellington. I wish you well."

Samantha again glanced down at her empty hands, the odd flutter of forgetting something tickled her brain as she strolled toward the ticket counter. She waited in line, watched other people check their luggage, and wrung her empty hands together. The last person in front of her stepped toward a ticket agent, and then she was waved forward. She retrieved Mr. Mason's envelope from her pocket and slid it open. She found a driver's license and a passport along with the cash—both euros and dollars—and her plane tickets. And she noticed another folded paper.

"Thank you, Miss Wellington, please take the escalator to terminal one, gate number nineteen. Your plane will begin loading in ten minutes. Security will take you a few minutes."

Rushing off, she followed the direction of the pointed finger. She unlaced her shoe in the security line, showed her ID and boarding pass, kicked off her shoe and went through the X-ray scanner—which took longer because of the boot. Slipping her foot back into her unlaced shoe, she loped to the gate and boarded the plane without stopping at the departure lounge. Irritation only added to her rapid breathing. Why hadn't Mr. Mason allotted more time? Her hollow uneven steps thudded down the gangplank, and she slipped through the door as an attendant closed it.

Another attendant greeted her at the aisle. "Welcome, can I help you find your seat?"

Samantha glanced down at her boarding pass, looking for the seat number.

The attendant peeked over the edge of the slip in her hand. "You are in first class, right this way." She led Samantha past the curtained section toward the front of the plane and motioned her to a seat near the window of the third row. A man in a business suit rose, allowing her access, and Samantha plopped down with a *humph*. Large seat, leg room—when did she become someone important? She snapped the belt and prepared for takeoff. It made her smile to wiggle her free foot in the ample space. She wouldn't be able to ride coach ever again. *And this is a far cry from a crate,* she snickered to herself.

London disappeared below her, and the Atlantic Ocean filled her window. Samantha rested her head on the plush seat and tipped it back as the plane reached altitude. She closed her eyes. A long flight over the ocean would pass faster if she could sleep, though after so long convalescing she wasn't really tired. The envelope brushed her hand as it slid down her lap. She snatched it from her knee before it fell and thumbed through the contents for the folded paper. She ran her finger over her name scrawled on the outside in block print. She opened it and read:

> dear samantha,
>
> i asked mase to pass this wee note on to you. i left you with too many words unsaid, luv.
>
> first, i want to apologize again for all the pain and suffering i have caused you. i would not want to see an innocent pay for me mistakes ever —but especially you, samantha. i never want to see you hurt again. but, luv, i have to say i don't regret meeting

you.

you be the best thing to ever happen to me. i know you don't want to believe it, but you be more intelligent than you believe. you be stronger than you think. you be more beautiful, capable, caring, passionate, and assured of yourself than you give yourself credit for, luv.

samantha, you be a rare jewel and any man who can't see your worth is a fool. i beseech the almighty to bring you a man who is worthy of you, but i know i am not that one. i am no good for you. i wish you all the best life can give you, luv.

be happy and be safe.
collin

A tear dripped on the letter, smearing part of Collin's signature. She swiped at her eyes with her jacket cuff, and dared a quick glance at the man next her. He sat with his head back and eyes closed, and she reread the letter. The second reading only brought more tears. When the flight attendant came around with drinks, she asked for tissues instead.

Folding the letter with care, after a fourth reading, she turned and stared out the window. White billowy clouds floated below. Their shapes shifted and changed like her hopes and dreams. She loved Collin for wanting to keep her safe, and railed at him because he couldn't see he was the man she needed most.

She laid her head back and allowed his words to wash over her like a warm ocean wave. *How will I go on without him?*

23 The Unbearable Normal

Samantha stepped off another plane in her
hometown, and lumbered down the jetbridge, her legs stiff
from sitting. Now how did she get home? She had no keys
to even get into her house once she got there. Through the
terminal and toward the escalator she wandered with slow,
labored steps. Maybe it didn't matter. The last she
remembered, her house was riddled with bullets. It might
be open to all the world. Did she even have a house to go
home to?

A man cleared his throat near her and she looked
up to focus on him. He inclined his head, and raised a sign
in his hand reading, "Samantha Wellington."

She blinked, read the sign again and looked at
him. He handed her a piece of paper. It was an email from
Mr. Mason asking his old friend, Gregory, to pick her up
and take her home. Her gaze narrowed on him for a
moment.

"Ol' Dec told me if you were not inclined to come
with me, I should tell you it is 2 a.m. in England, but he
would still do a video chat if you needed—his wife
wouldn't be happy though."

Samantha looked at him for a moment. He could
be lying. But who else knew she had only trusted Mr.

Mason after a Facetime conversation with Collin. He had to be telling the truth didn't he?

The man pulled out his wallet from his back pocket, as Samantha watched his every move. He removed a dog-eared old photo and handed it to her. She smiled at the silly fishing hats and vests worn by a much younger Mr. Mason next to a youthful version of the man in front of her. She let out a slow breath as she handed it back. "No, don't wake him. I'd hate for his wife to be further upset with him," she said, recalling their conversations in the hospital of how Mrs. Mason disliked the hours of his job—though she didn't really know what he did.

Gregory waved his arm and she fell into step alongside him as they walked across the street and into the parking structure to his car. Their steps echoed off the cement walls and clanged on the metal stairs. An odd chill crept up her arms. She slipped into the passenger seat, and they proceeded to her house, the radio humming country music to fill the time. As they stopped into her driveway he turned to her and placed keys in her hands—her keys. "You might be needing these."

She looked at him, confused, but he just smiled and wished her well. Rounding the garage that protruded out from the rest of the house, she approached the front door. There were no broken windows, the security screen looked different. The walls were all intact—no bullet holes in the stucco. *The house had been shot up—right?*

The key turned the lock with a familiar clank and she opened the screen and unlocked the front door with a pop of the lock. Furniture sat out of place and some of it she had never seen before. The fumes of fresh paint filled the space, making her dizzy. She found her bed made. Was the mattress new? *It sat taller than that—didn't it?* The closet doors, now white wood instead of brown metal, made the room feel brighter.

She kicked off her shoe at the foot of the bed. The new carpet squished more under her stocking foot. She turned to the office across the hall. The last time she'd stood here, half the glass was gone from the windows and Collin squeezed her neck until she passed out.

Now the blinds were down. Opening them showed a whole window. Everything had been repaired or replaced.

Grateful to whoever had fixed everything, she moved to the couch and plopped down. *Now what?*

After a few hours and a nap, Samantha snatched up her purse from its place on the floor near the front door and her keys and went to the store for food. Returning home, she called her principal to see if she still had a job. Christmas break would start in another couple of days, and plans were made for her to return at the first of the year.

Samantha called other friends and family, answered a thousand questions with her prepared explanation, and settled into an unbearably quiet and dull life. It was what her life had always been—but now it wasn't enough.

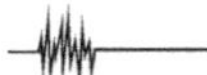

Samantha flipped on the air conditioner and plopped down in her recliner with a home-made smoothie. She sighed, clicking off the TV and the rerun of some series she'd seen a thousand times. Reaching for her eReader, she tried to distract herself from her boring life. She set it on her lap but didn't turn it on. Life after Collin still felt like no life at all.

She'd returned for the second semester with her students, and they all acted like they were glad to have her back—the other teachers too. Teaching occupied her days, but her nights were an endless drudgery and her lonely brain considered leaping off trains and dodging bullets somehow preferable to nights alone in front of the TV. Now, with school out for the summer, her house felt more like solitary confinement than a home.

Not that she was ever really alone. From the time she returned, two utility trucks had taken up permanent residence in her neighborhood. The power truck always sat on her street and the phone van lived on the street out her front door that ran perpendicular to hers. She didn't know who they were—SIS, FBI, CIA—but they were always there. No one else in the neighborhood seemed to notice them. Other familiar vehicles shadowed her to work and the store. Some nameless government entity always remained within earshot, and she figured her house was bugged with listening devices too. Were they as bored with her life as she was?

She tossed the eReader aside and took out Collin's letter again. The folds were thin and barely holding together from her constant opening and closing of it. She considered slipping it into a plastic page protector, but she liked the feel of the paper Collin had once touched in her fingers. She read the tear-stained paper again, and let out a long slow sigh. Her arms sat limp in her lap— like dead fish on the sand. Wasn't it just her luck to finally find the man of her dreams only to have no chance of being with him? She refolded the paper, unable to stifle another sigh.

The doorbell rang.

Opening the door, she peered through the security screen to a bunch of live flowers in a wooden basket, above brown shorts and pale legs. She couldn't see a face.

"Afternoon, ma'am. Got a delivery for ya."

"I didn't order flowers," she said glancing for the phone van. It still sat there, but she had no way of knowing if anyone sat inside—or if they were even still alive.

"Perhaps ya have one of them secret 'mirers."

He kept standing at the door, but never let his face show through the arrangement. Samantha shifted her weight from one foot to the other. *Do I dare open the door? Isn't this how victims always get tricked in the movies—opening the door to some random deliveryman?*

"Ya want me to leave it out here in the heat, ma'am? Them's awful nice buds."

She glanced again at her surveillance and decided to chance it. If he was going to shoot her, he could do so easily through the webbed security screen between them. If he tried to gab her, she'd try some of her new self-defense training on him. With the large flower basket in his hands, it didn't seem likely he would have much luck getting his hands on her anyway. And it would at least be something different in her ho-hum day.

Samantha planted her feet, ready if he tried anything, and reached for the lock. "No, I'll take them." Her heart beat harder as she turned the deadbolt in the screen. Samantha pushed it open but held onto the knob at the ready to yank it closed if he reached for her.

He stepped back putting her at some ease.

Still holding Collin's letter, she reached for the basket, but it was heavier then she could hold so she braced her right shoulder against the doorframe and took the plant in both hands.

The deliveryman's hand brushed over hers, and warmth rippled through her entire body. She tensed, at the ready for his next move.

He pressed her hands tighter against the basket to assure it didn't fall. "Ya have yourself a fine day, ma'am."

No threat tainted his words, and she allowed the breath she held to ease away. She lowered the basket to look over it at the deliveryman, but he held the brim of his brown ball cap in front of his face as he tipped it at her.

Samantha waited and watched.

His head remained hidden below the bill when he replaced the cap.

As he turned toward his delivery van, she caught a glimpse of his face. *Crooked smile?* Her heart leapt in her throat, strangling her and keeping her from calling out Collin's name. She watched his every step, all the way to the van. *Is that Collin's walk?* She closed her eyes as the van drove away. *Were there freckles around that familiar smile?*

She shook her head and her arms dropped to hold the basket below her waist. *You want to see him so bad, you silly woman, now you're imagining you see him everywhere.* She stepped back inside, balanced the flowers and yanked the security screen closed with a bang.

Locking it again, she gathered the arrangement and kicked the door closed. She set the flowers on her kitchen table, scanned it for listening devices, and drew a card from within their petals.

She tugged it free from the plastic stake and her heart skipped a beat at the familiar block script of her name written diagonally across the tiny square envelope. She tore it open, read the four words written within, and clutched the card to her pounding heart.

Leave the window open.

About the Author

Michelle Janene (Murray) is a full-time teacher and
a writer. Her writings are included
in 5 Inspire Christian Writers Anthologies. She has
won honors in new writers contests.
She leads both an adult and a student writing group
to grow and encourage other writers.

Michelle lives in Northern California, with two
crazy dogs and a host of characters from her
imagination.

Visit Michelle:

StrongTowerPress.com

Find Michelle Janene Turret Writing on Facebook
Or Strong Tower Press on Facebook

Follow @MichelleJaneneM on Twitter